Something had created a strange sense of intimacy between them, even though they were nearly strangers.

She wished she knew what it was. She tipped her chin down, trying to find the right words to ask.

He nudged it back up with a forefinger, and the contact sent a buzz through her system. "Why did you run?"

The look in his eyes stripped away her pretenses, leaving her with the bare truth. "Because I wasn't strong enough to resist you and I knew it. It would have been a disaster for both of us. Why don't you see it? What do you remember about that night that I don't?"

A look of pain, or maybe resignation crossed his handsome features. "This."

And he kissed her.

JESSICA ANDERSEN

RAPID FIRE

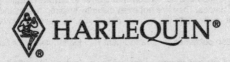

HARLEQUIN®

TORONTO • NEW YORK • LONDON
AMSTERDAM • PARIS • SYDNEY • HAMBURG
STOCKHOLM • ATHENS • TOKYO • MILAN • MADRID
PRAGUE • WARSAW • BUDAPEST • AUCKLAND

ISBN-13: 978-0-373-88702-6
ISBN-10: 0-373-88702-7

RAPID FIRE

www.eHarlequin.com

Printed in U.S.A.

ABOUT THE AUTHOR

Though she's tried out professions ranging from cleaning sea lion cages to cloning glaucoma genes, from patent law to training horses, Jessica is happiest when she's combining all these interests with her first love: writing romances. These days she's delighted to be writing full-time on a farm in rural Connecticut that she shares with a small menagerie and a hero named Brian. She hopes you'll visit her at www.JessicaAndersen.com for info on upcoming books, contests and to say "hi"!

Books by Jessica Andersen

HARLEQUIN INTRIGUE

*Bear Claw Creek Crime Lab

Don't miss any of our special offers. Write to us at the following address for information on our newest releases.

Harlequin Reader Service
U.S.: 3010 Walden Ave., P.O. Box 1325, Buffalo, NY 14269
Canadian: P.O. Box 609, Fort Erie, Ont. L2A 5X3

CAST OF CHARACTERS

Maya Cooper—Suspended from the Bear Claw Crime Lab, the psych specialist is alone in believing that a local philanthropist is responsible for the crime wave currently terrorizing Bear Claw City. Her only ally is a dangerous man from her past.

Thorne Coleridge—Some cops say he has "powers." Others think he's a brilliantly intuitive profiler. Thorne himself knows two things about the current case: one, Maya is the only woman who can save him from himself, and two, loving him could mean her death.

Wexton Henkes—The local legend stands accused of heinous crimes. How far will he go to protect himself?

Alissa Wyatt & Cassie Dumont—The other members of the Bear Claw Crime Lab try to protect Maya by shutting her out of the investigation.

Detectives Piedmont & Montoya—The partners have been openly hostile to the three women of the new crime lab.

Nevada Barnes—The museum murderer tries to cut a deal from prison. Can he be trusted?

Chief Parry—Bear Claw's police chief is under huge pressure to catch the criminal mastermind. When a suspended cop becomes the fiend's next target, will he bow to pressure and use her as bait?

Drew Wilson—When two police sketches help identify him as a suspect, he will do anything to avoid capture.

Prologue

He stood on a bluff overlooking green summer pastures and raised a pair of binoculars to his eyes as the morning sun climbed above the opposite ridgetop.

The target lay in the valley below, a jumble of Hollywood-false Western buildings and swirling bison herds. It would be so easy this time.

Almost too easy.

At the beginning, when he'd first conceived his revenge, he'd thought of himself as the planner. The cops had christened him the Mastermind, because he'd so carefully organized his strategy and found men to do his bidding. Bradford Croft had been pliable, with a fondness for young girls that had made him easy to direct. Nevada Barnes had been less malleable. More angry. More dangerous. But he, too, had his weaknesses.

Croft was dead now and Barnes was in jail, but the plan lived on. Divide and conquer.

Revenge. Retribution.

The Mastermind tightened his fingers on the binoculars as a school bus lumbered into view below, passing beneath a swinging sign that promised authentic Wild West entertainment.

Children spilled from the bus and their shrill, excited voices filtered up to his vantage point. Then the adults emerged, moving more slowly, thinking themselves safe. The Canyon Kidnapper was dead and the Museum Murderer—an epithet he blamed solely on the media—was in jail. The citizens of Bear Claw, Colorado, thought the danger was past.

They had no idea it was just beginning.

Chapter One

Wearing jeans and a fitted blue T-shirt on her lean, five-foot-nothing frame, with her dark hair tucked beneath a straw hat and a canvas bag slung over her shoulder, Maya Cooper looked every inch the tourist she'd intended to portray. But inside, she was all cop as she scanned the swept-clean brick roadway that ran down the center of the faux ghost town outside Bear Claw City.

Her training as a criminal profiler told her she was reaching, but her gut told her she was on to something.

She was positive the Chuckwagon Ranch was connected to the sick bastard who'd planned two separate violent crime sprees over the past six months.

Wexton Henkes, part owner of the theme park, was a Bear Claw legend. Born in the city and raised up through the school system, he'd taken his father's one-room electronic repair shop and built it into an empire. Once he'd made his first million—or ten—he'd started giving back to the city that had brought him his success. He'd funded everything from civic projects and art revivals to nature conservation and the local sports teams. In short, he was a prince.

On the outside, at least. Inside, Maya was convinced he was something else entirely. He'd broken his own son's arm three months earlier—nobody could tell her different—and he was poised to duck the abuse charges because he had money, power and influence.

Enough influence to get her in serious trouble the last time she'd gone after him.

"But not this time," she said aloud, earning herself strange looks from the passing tourists.

The June morning was warm and bright, perfect for a family trip. The Wild West theme park was cut down the middle by Main Street, a wide brick causeway flanked with false-fronted buildings that had been painted to look like a saloon, a general store and a livery. Tourists streamed into and out of the buildings in a chaos of movement and sound that made it almost impossible to pick out individuals. On either side of the buildings, bison-dotted pastures stretched for miles, taking up most of the shallow, hill-bounded bowl of land.

Maya scanned the low ridgetops that flanked the road and saw nothing. A faint feeling of wrongness prickled at the nape of her neck, a familiar sense of being watched. Of being alone.

But damn it, she *was* alone. She'd been suspended from the Bear Claw Police Department pending an inquiry into the incident at the Henkes mansion three months earlier.

Anxiety pressed at her, echoing her heartbeat in the low-grade headache that had plagued her ever since she'd awoken in the Hawthorne Hospital with a knot on the back of her head and no memory of attacking Henkes in his own home.

But that was what she'd done. Or so they said.

What if they kicked her off the force? Maya's throat closed at the thought. She was already on the outside of the Bear Claw City Police Department—BCCPD—looking in.

Alissa Wyatt and Cassie Dumont, her best friends and coworkers within the start-up Forensics Department, had tried to include her in the gossip, but they were run ragged shouldering her work as well as their own.

The new three-woman forensics team was struggling to gain acceptance within the Bear Claw PD as it was. What if—

No, Maya told herself, she wouldn't dwell on that. The previous night she'd finally decided it was time to stop with the futile attempts at self-hypnosis, the painful efforts to force some remembrance of that night at the Henkes mansion. It was no use. The memories were gone, and she had an ugly feeling she knew why.

She touched a hand to her throat, where her charm necklace held five bangles. There should have been six more, but she'd lost them to a mistake. To temptation.

Would she lose the remaining five charms as well?

What if she had to start over again?

"No," she said aloud. "I'm stronger than that, and I'm damn well going to prove it. Starting now."

As though on cue, her cell phone rang, a

digital bleat that cracked through the background hum of tourism. Not expecting a call, Maya slapped open the unit and checked the number, but the ID was blocked.

Annoyed, she flipped the phone shut and dropped it in the front pocket of her canvas bag. These days most of her calls came from media hounds looking for quotes on the dismissal of the Henkes child-abuse trial, or supporters of Wexton Henkes himself calling to threaten her, somehow still believing the bastard had a solid shot at the upcoming Congressional election. She didn't need to talk to either group.

Focused on her own special way of doing the job—more organic than straight detecting, more regimented than pure profiling— she followed the flow of tourists toward the livery building, which held a petting zoo.

She wanted to get a feel for the theme park and the man who'd bankrolled it.

Inside the building, rough-hewn boards and crooked center beams gave the sense of an old, run-down barn, though a closer look showed her that everything was neat and new, and painted to look old. The place was packed with excited children, along with adults wearing expressions that ranged from enthusiasm to exhaustion. Small goats and lambs wandered a straw-bedded center pen, begging for handfuls of pellets that could be bought from quarter-operated machines on the wall. Box stalls on either side were set up to hold larger animals, though only one was occupied, holding a shaggy bison that looked close to five feet tall at the shoulder and probably weighed in well over a thousand pounds. Its short, curved horns were dulled at the ends, but that did little to blunt the physical impact of the creature as it snorted and stomped in its enclosure.

Maya noted the people and animals, then turned her attention to the building. She wasn't even sure what she was looking for. A sense of the place, maybe, or insight into the man who had financial ties not only to the ranch, but also to the state park where Alissa had found the kidnapped girls during the first crime wave, and to the Bear Claw Natural History Museum where Cassie had nearly lost her life in the second.

During her terrifying ordeal in the museum, Cassie had heard the computer-altered voice of a third man, one who called himself the planner.

He had promised more violence to come.

The members of the special BCCPD task force assembled to deal with the crimes had vowed to find the Mastermind before he could strike again, but their leads had fizzled out in the months since. They needed an accurate psychological profile of the criminal, but their quarry was too many things and none of them all at once. It was nearly impossible to separate his ego from the works of the men he'd coerced into executing the actual crimes, but Maya was damn sure going to try.

So what if she was off the case, off the force entirely? That didn't stop her from being a cop. Didn't stop her from wanting to prove that she wasn't—

The phone rang again, startling her. Though the ID was still blocked, she stepped outside the petting zoo and answered it, planning to give the persistent journalist an earful. "Maya Cooper speaking. Who is this?"

"You don't know me," said an eerie, mechanized voice.

A jolt slapped through her. The distorted sound matched Cassie's description of the Mastermind's voice.

She swallowed and said, "Hello, Wexton. How's the arm?"

She was sure of her suspect. She just had to convince the rest of the BCCPD.

Dead silence echoed over the digital airwaves. For a moment she thought he'd hung up. Then the mechanized voice returned. "You think you're so smart, don't you? Well, I've got a surprise for you."

Maya's fingers tightened on the cell phone. "What kind of surprise?"

The voice held a hint of metallic amusement when it said, "There's a bomb hidden somewhere in the Chuckwagon Ranch. You have ten minutes to evacuate."

"YOU WANT ME TO DO *WHAT?*" Thorne Coleridge stopped pacing the small office and stared at Bear Claw City's Police Chief.

William Parry, grizzled and bulldogesque with his jowly face and sad eyes, leaned back in his desk chair. "Do you want the job or not?"

Thorne jammed his hands in the pockets of the navy wool slacks he'd worn as a concession to the interview. He'd gotten a quick trim of his short, sandy hair and donned a white oxford-cloth shirt, but had skipped the tie, figuring he should begin as he meant to go on.

The question echoed in his brain. Did he want the job? Did he want to get in at the ground level of a start-up forensics department? Hell, yes. Did he want to get out of the Wagon Ridge PD, where conversations stopped the moment he entered the room and the whispers began the moment he left? Hell, yes. That was why he'd jumped at the chance when his bosses in Wagon Ridge had asked if he would drive down to Bear Claw and help with an ongoing case. He needed a fresh start.

But he wasn't sure he wanted to make that start at the expense of a colleague.

He resumed his pacing before he said, "Nobody told me I'd be replacing another psych specialist. I thought you were looking to fill a vacancy."

"It can become a vacancy if you do your job. Hell, I'll probably have to replace her either way." But Parry's frown drooped lower, cutting deeper lines in his sagging face. "The three women came with glowing references and wanted to work together. I was looking to upgrade my forensics team. It seemed like a match."

"I take it things haven't gone smoothly?"

Parry snorted. "You could say that. If it isn't one thing with those three, it's another. At first, they couldn't manage to get along with the rest of the PD. They did their jobs well enough, but it was tense as hell. Then once all this trouble started, my crime scene expert and my evidence tech wound up snuggling with my best detective and my FBI liaison." His expression darkened. "Hell, they wound up being targeted by the damn killer!"

"You can't blame them for the criminal mind," Thorne said, avoiding the touchy issue of inter-departmental romance. He didn't need to go there. Not now.

Not ever again.

"True, but whether it's their fault or not, things have been unsettled in the PD since they came on board." The chief shifted in his chair. "Then add on this business with Wexton Henkes…" He trailed off, but his sour expression left no doubt that he'd had it with his crack team of investigators. "My so-called psych specialist accused Bear

Claw's biggest philanthropist of child abuse—against the sworn testimony of his wife and son, mind you—and then attacked him in his own home before she collapsed and remained unconscious for nearly three days." Parry muttered a curse. "I just don't think she's an asset to the PD at this point. I'd like to replace her with someone more stable. More qualified."

Thorne grimaced. Surely the rumors had traveled down to Bear Claw, stories of how he'd gone up into the mountains after cult leader Mason Falk, and how he'd been a changed man afterwards.

But maybe the chief figured that was a long time ago, and knew he'd proven himself since.

God knows he'd tried to.

He thought of the opportunity he was being offered. A fresh start, away from—

Well, just away.

Interest piqued, Thorne withdrew his hands from his pockets and sat in the padded chair facing the chief's desk. He gestured toward the glass wall separating the chief's office from the bulk of the Bear Claw PD, where cops worked in their cubes or hustled out on calls. "What about the others? Won't they see me as just as much of an intruder? Hell, what about the women? They're going to hate me if I break up their cozy little unit."

"They'll deal," the chief said bluntly, though Thorne caught a flicker of doubt in his eyes. "Alissa Wyatt is the crime scene analyst. Does sketches, too. She's engaged to Detective Tucker McDermott, Homicide. Make friends with Tucker and she'll tolerate you. Cassie Dumont is our evidence tech. She paired off with Seth Varitek, an FBI evidence specialist out of the Boulder office. She'll be tougher, and won't care whether you make nice with Seth or not. If I were you, I'd just stay out of her way while you work this case." The chief leaned forward in his chair and pinned Thorne with a no-nonsense look. "Here's the deal. I'm putting you on the Mastermind task force. We need a solid profile and a new direction, and we need it yesterday, before this bastard attacks my city again. Consider this case your job interview. You fit in here and help us catch the Mastermind, and the job's yours."

Thorne nodded as a stir of anticipation drowned out most of his doubts. "I'll need copies of the case files, all the notes your investigators have amassed on the Canyon Kidnappings and the Museum Murders, everything that pertains to the Mastermind."

"The computer files and hard copies are waiting for you downstairs in the forensics department offices. You'll have to share with Alissa and Cassie, I'm afraid, but maybe that's for the best. It'll let you three get used to each other." The chief stood and extended his hand, indicating that the interview—such as it had been—was over. "I expect interesting things from you, Coleridge. Don't let me down."

As Thorne stood and shook with the man who would be—at least temporarily—his new superior, he saw the knowledge in Parry's eyes and heard the emphasis on the word *interesting*. That was enough to tell him that the chief had heard the rumors about his so-called talents, after all. Maybe that explained why he'd called Wagon Ridge and asked for Thorne personally.

Yeah, that was it, he decided. The chief was hoping he'd provide a miracle.

Too bad he'd have to disappoint.

"I'll do my best police work," he said carefully.

The chief paused, then nodded. "You do that."

It wasn't until Thorne turned for the door that he saw the commotion outside, heard the muted shouts in the bullpen. Adrenaline spurted. "What the hell?"

A woman yanked open the door before he could reach for it. Medium height with honey-blond hair pulled into a ponytail beneath a BCCPD ball cap, she had deep blue eyes that were wide with stress, though she kept her voice professionally level when she said, "He's back. We just had a bomb threat phoned in to that bison park outside the city. Computerized voice and all."

"The Mastermind phoned here?" the chief demanded, already shrugging into his jacket.

The woman shook her head. "Worse. He called Maya's cell."

The chief repeated the name like a curse, but the word froze Thorne to his core.

"Maya?" he said, and something must have leaked into his voice because the woman and Chief Parry both turned to him.

"Maya Cooper," the chief said. "The psych specialist that you're re—that you're subbing for while she's on suspension."

The sudden darkening of the woman's eyes told Thorne the chief's slip hadn't gone unnoticed. She glared at Parry, then at Thorne, but said only, "I'm out of here. We've got a bomb to find and a scene to process. Everything else will have to wait."

She slammed the door behind her, making the glass shudder.

The chief paused with his hand on the knob and turned to Thorne. "That was Alissa, the friendlier of your two new coworkers. Sounds like you're going to have problems."

"I can handle it," Thorne said carefully, but the chief had no idea how right he was in predicting a problem.

It wasn't Alissa he was worried about, though.

It was Maya.

Chapter Two

"Everybody stay calm. It's all under control." Though her heart pounded in her chest, Maya pitched her voice low as the crowd of tourists she'd collected in the parking lot outside the ranch edged toward panic. "The police will be here soon to check on the *possibility*," she stressed the last word, though in her mind there was no doubt the Mastermind had been deadly serious, "that there's a problem."

The tourists and ranch employees milled in a bare area beyond the parking lot, shifting restlessly as though they had ceased to be single individuals and become a combined entity, a spooky, nervous mob that could stampede at any moment.

Maya strained to hear the sound of approaching sirens even as she raised her hands.

"Please stay calm. It'll just be a few more minutes."

A few minutes until the Bear Claw cops arrived. A few minutes until the bomb detonated, minutes that ticked down on the digital display of her wristwatch.

The explosive could be in any one of the buildings. Or it could be in one of the cars. Even in the big yellow school bus parked in the corner of the lot, Maya thought with a faint shudder as the numbers clicked down from five minutes to four.

"Let's get in the cars and get out of here," a man's voice called, and others shouted agreement.

"I'm sorry, that's not an option." Maya glanced to her right and left, where two terrified-looking ranch employees were helping her keep the group in check now that the initial rush to get people the hell out of the ranch had passed. The three of them were holding the line, but the crowd could turn at a moment's notice.

Maya had studied mob mentality. She'd been in situations like this before.

But back then, she'd had a badge and a weapon, and street cops backing her up.

"Why not?" shouted the same voice, irritated now. "And who put you in charge?"

She glared in the direction of the heckler. "I'm a member of the Bear Claw Creek Police Department, which puts me in charge."

She didn't give her name, because it had already been splashed too loudly in the media, and she didn't give her rank or show her badge, because she'd been stripped of both until Internal Affairs finished looking into the Henkes incident, a process that had been stalled several times by red tape she could only assume came from Henkes's supporters within the force.

Three minutes, thirty seconds.

She tried not to think about her first impressions of the theme park, how a sniper could sit up on the low ridge of hills nearby and fire down into the crowd she had assembled in a too-convenient knot. But what other choice did she have? She'd needed to get them the hell out of the park, and the vehicles weren't an option.

Three minutes.

Then she heard sirens in the distance, approaching rapidly.

"Thank God," Maya whispered to herself, knowing she couldn't say it aloud, couldn't let the crowd know she was worried.

They needed her to be strong, to keep the peace.

Precious seconds ticked by as the Bear Claw cops pulled in, led by Alissa and Cassie, riding with Tucker in his he-man truck. The chief's car followed moments later. The sight of her friends loosened the tight band around Maya's heart, even as the suspicious looks she got from the other arriving officers made her feel worse.

Uniforms ranged out around the rapidly quieting crowd. As the tension subsided a degree, a youngish cop jogged over to Maya and said, "We'll take it from here, ma'am. The chief would like a word with you."

She tried not to wince at the "ma'am," which served only to underscore her status as not-quite-a-cop. But there wasn't time for regrets, not while her wristwatch clicked down past two minutes thirty seconds.

She hastened to the knot of cops gathered near the chief's car just as two vans and a box truck arrived in a cloud of dust, bearing John Sawyer, the leader of the Bear Claw Bomb Squad, along with his team of experts.

"He said I had ten minutes," she told the group. "We've got two-thirty left, give or take. The park is cleared of people, but there's a petting zoo in the livery building and close to three hundred head of bison pastured right behind the buildings."

"Not much we can do about that now," Chief Parry said pragmatically, but his grizzled, careworn face settled into deeper lines at the prospect of bloodshed, human or otherwise. When Sawyer joined the group, the chief quickly updated him. The two put their heads together to rough out a plan, which gave Maya a moment to glance at the others.

Alissa's honey-blond hair was tied back in a ponytail and stuffed under a navy BCCPD ball cap, while Cassie's straight, nearly white-blond hair was shorter now, cut near her shoulders. Tucker stood just behind Alissa and off to one side, shoulders stiff and protective. A wolf guarding his mate. Knowing that the task force had remained active even after the capture of Nevada Barnes three months earlier, Maya was faintly surprised by the absence of Special Agent Seth Varitek. Cassie's nemesis-turned-lover had been loaned to the task force for help with the evidence work, but perhaps he was off on another case.

In Varitek's place, a stranger stood at the edge of the group, part of the conversation but apart from the center of it. He was maybe a shade over six feet tall, lean but muscular. He wore navy pants and a crisp white shirt at odds with the heavy boots on his feet. His close-cropped sandy hair was standard military, as was his stiff-backed posture, and she sensed him studying her from behind his dark sunglasses.

She felt a shimmer of familiarity. A cold crawl moved across her shoulders and up her neck to gather at the base of her skull.

Who was this guy?

Her watch beeped to indicate sixty seconds left in the countdown. Thirty.

In silent accord, the cops turned toward the Chuckwagon Ranch as the seconds bled away. There was no way they could search the entire place in time. They didn't even know where to begin.

As the final few seconds ran down on the digital display, Chief Parry nodded to Maya. "Good work getting everyone out. They're safe, thanks to you."

It was the first time he'd spoken to her since he'd taken her badge. The recognition warmed her, but she said, "I was just doing my job."

Then the time ran out. Her watch beeped the end of the promised ten minutes. They braced for an explosion.

Nothing happened.

Seconds ticked by. Then minutes. Still nothing.

Maya's brain sped up. Her thoughts quickened to a blur, but it was Sawyer who said, "Think it's another dud?"

During the Museum Murder investigation, Cassie's house had been rigged with a gas leak and a detonator that hadn't triggered. Sawyer later determined that it had never been intended to blow. It'd been a fake, designed to confuse them. Scare them.

Could this be the same?

"It would fit with the Mastermind's pattern," Maya said quietly. "Hell, there might not even be a device. He probably got off on phoning in a threat and watching us scramble."

She told herself not to be ashamed by the false alarm. There was no way she could have known, no way she could have chanced ignoring the call.

But still, she squirmed at the sidelong glances of her former coworkers and the stranger in the dark glasses.

Sawyer gestured to his team. "We'll suit up and search the property to make sure. It'll take a few hours."

"With all due respect," Maya said, "I'd suggest you check the vehicles first. The tourists are pretty edgy to leave."

"With all due respect," the chief said, "you should go with them. The media will be here any minute. If they catch wind that you're involved with this bomb scare, the next thing we know, it'll be splashed across the six o'clock news. Suspended cop receives bomb tip. Film at eleven. Hell, they'll want to know why you received the call. Is it because you're the last Forensics Department cop to be targeted? Or maybe it's completely unrelated. Maybe this is about the Henkes trial next week. Lord knows, you've ticked off more than a few people with that."

His words dug at Maya's suspicions, at the places she hadn't yet managed to armor. "That would make it completely related," she snapped. "Why do you think I was here in the first place? Henkes is—"

"He's right," Alissa interrupted, though her voice was laced with apology when she said, "You should go. Leave your cell phone with us for analysis. Tucker and I will swing by your place later to get a full statement."

Ouch. Maya fought the wince, crossed her arms and nodded tightly. "Of course. I'm sorry." She forced the words through a throat gone tight with resentment.

Was this what she'd been reduced to? Waiting at home for her friends to drop by with a crumb of information?

When nobody argued, she swallowed the anger and pushed through the group. Her path brought her between Alissa and the stranger.

Alissa touched Maya's arm and mouthed, "I'm sorry. We'll talk later."

The stranger just looked down at her through his shaded lenses with an intensity that set off warning bells.

Maya had the wild, uncharacteristic urge to reach up and pull those glasses down so she could see his eyes. But wild urges were self-destructive. She knew that much from experience. So she sniffed and pushed past him, bumping his arm with hers to let him know she wasn't intimidated.

Damned if he didn't flinch.

THE FLASH CAME THE MOMENT she touched him.

Blood. Death. Violence. Heat. Thorne held himself rigid and weathered the sensations, which were part memory, part anticipation. He gritted his teeth and forced himself not to show the whiplash of mental flame, of pain.

Hell, he thought when she was gone and the images faded, *what was that?*

It was a stupid question. He knew precisely what it had been. But why here? Why now? It had been years since his last vision, years since the doctors had assured him the flashes were nothing more than random synapse firings, courtesy of the drugs he'd been given during his captivity on Mason Falk's mountain.

Years since he'd blocked the images, which had often come too close to prescience for his comfort.

He rubbed the place on his arm that she'd touched, where the contact had arced through the fabric of his shirt and punched him in the gut with the flash.

Or had that been nothing more than memory of their brief history?

She hadn't recognized him. He shouldn't have been surprised, given how much he'd changed since his brief stint teaching at the High Top Bluff Police Academy. His hair had been long then, and he'd been weak from the aftereffects of his captivity. Twitchy from the post-traumatic stress. He'd taken his first drink at ten each morning, and spaced five more whiskeys out through the day, staying sober enough to teach his classes, buzzed enough to avoid the memories. The visions.

He didn't remember much about the half year after his captivity, but he remembered her. The moment he'd heard her name again after all these years, an image of her face had sprung into his mind full-blown.

Now, seeing her in person, he realized that she hadn't changed a bit. She was still tiny, with every piece of her perfectly proportioned, just as she'd been when she'd taken his Advanced Criminal Psych class. Her dark hair was styled differently, hanging to her shoulders now in soft waves, but the face below was the same as he'd remembered, making him wonder whether the image in his mind had been memory or something born of another power, one he'd fought to block for nearly five years now.

He shoved his hands in his pockets and turned to watch her make her way down to the parking lot, shoulders tense beneath her blue short-sleeved shirt.

How could she still look the same when he was so different?

A phone rang, startling him with its strident digital peal.

"You take it." The chief tossed him Maya's cell.

Thorne caught it on the fly as it rang a second time. He struggled to refocus, to bring his wayward brain back from places it had no business being. His voice was gruff when he said, "Wouldn't it be better to have one of the women answer and pretend to be Dr. Cooper?"

Parry shook his head. "He'll know. During the other cases, he spliced a line into the PD security cameras so he could watch us at headquarters. Same thing at the museum when Barnes was captured. He'll be watching somehow. You can bet on it."

Accepting that, Thorne flipped open the

phone and punched it to speaker before he said, "Hello?"

There was a pause—a long, thin stretch of silence with absolutely nothing on the other end.

"Hello?" Thorne prompted again, aware of the others watching him.

There was still no answer. Moments later, the call was disconnected.

Thorne muttered a curse. "Nothing." He shook his head and returned the phone to Chief Parry, who had his own cell in his hand, perhaps to call in reinforcements at any hint of a break in the case.

Parry held Thorne's eyes. "Nothing at all?"

Knowing what the chief was asking, Thorne shoved his hands in his pockets. "I'm a cop, not a magician."

Before the chief could respond, Sawyer's voice crackled from a nearby radio. "We've done a quick scan and we haven't found a thing."

"There's no bomb?" the chief said quickly.

Sawyer's transmitted voice responded, "I can't be entirely certain until we've done a more thorough search. With explosives technology being what it is, a charge could be hidden anywhere. But the other devices this guy used were all pretty standard—none of the molded polymers or really high-power stuff. If he's sticking with the pattern, I'd expect to find a fairly traditional device. But we've got nothing here. Nada."

"Keep looking." But when the chief lowered the radio, his expression was pensive. He glanced over at Thorne. "With what you know of him so far, would the Mastermind go to a more advanced explosive?"

"In my opinion?" Thorne stressed the last word, trying to remind the Bear Claw chief that he didn't specialize in parlor tricks. "I don't think so. Granted, part of his pattern is that he has very little pattern, but I'd say he has an ego. He wants to be feared, wants to be seen as the best. If he had more advanced technological abilities, I think he would've used them already. That leaves us three possibilities."

The tall blond bombshell who'd been introduced to him as the evidence specialist, Cassie Dumont, raised her eyebrows. "Which are?"

Her prickly tone indicated that she had no intention of liking him.

Thorne answered, "Well, the first option is that our mastermind is playing with us again, that he phoned in a false threat just to watch us scramble. If so, we need to address the question of why he phoned Officer Cooper." It felt odd to use her title, but it would be equally awkward to use her name for the first time in five years, for the first time since he'd woken up and found her gone after their one strange, disjointed night together.

They'd meant nothing to each other, yet she'd changed his life. A better man would thank her for it.

Instead, Thorne was lined up to take her job.

"He's targeted her because she's a woman," said the lean, rangy cop who'd identified himself as Detective Tucker McDermott, Homicide, "and because she's a member of the Forensics Department."

"Maybe," Thorne said. "Or maybe there's something else going on here. Option number two is that—regardless of the mech-anized voice, which seems to indicate the Mastermind—this could be about a different case entirely."

Cassie scowled. "Henkes."

"Right," Thorne said. The chief had brought him up to speed on the case during the ride to the ranch. "What if one of his supporters is trying to discredit her?"

"Then they're a bunch of idiots," Cassie snapped. "Maya's reputation is impeccable."

Except for the part where she was suspended for accosting a suspect without proper procedure or backup, Thorne thought, but didn't say it aloud because the psych specialist's friends were going to like his third possibility even less.

The chief must have sensed his reluctance, because he said, "And the third possibility?"

Thorne tried not to feel a beat of empathy when he said, "Maybe there was no bomb threat in the first place."

He'd expected Cassie to blast him, and was mildly surprised when it was Alissa who got in his face in a single smooth, nearly deadly move. She didn't raise her voice, but her tone was chilly when she said, "What, precisely, are you implying? Are you saying that Maya—logical, grounded, patient Maya—phoned in a fake bomb threat?"

He glanced down toward the parking area. Sawyer's men must have cleared the vehicles to leave, because he saw a gaggle of kids being herded back onto a school bus. Unerringly, his eyes were drawn to the dainty, dark-haired figure of a woman standing near another woman, apparently deep in conversation.

"Nobody knows precisely what happened that night. All we know for sure is that Henkes was shot with Officer Cooper's weapon," he said, more to himself than to the others. "What if…"

He trailed off as he saw her peel away from the others down in the parking lot and head toward the main park entrance.

"What if?" the chief prompted.

"Never mind. I'll be right back." Without waiting for the chief's okay, Thorne picked his way down to the main parking lot. He wasn't sure what prompted him to follow her—curiosity, maybe, or the memory of the strange flash he'd experienced when she'd brushed past him. But as he hopped over the turnstile and tried to figure out which way she'd turned on the deserted main street, he felt an unfamiliar, unwanted prickling in his brain.

Danger.

"HANNAH?" SEEING NO SIGNS of the little girl who had slipped away from her mother out in the parking lot, Maya cursed under her breath and turned down a cross street toward the pony rides.

She'd promised to find the child, wanting to keep the mother outside, where it was supposedly safe.

Now she wondered whether she should have passed off the request to one of the uniforms, someone with a gun and backup, just in case.

She heard the bellows of agitated bison from the other side of the buildings. According to the ranch hands, the police sirens and unusual activity in the park had upset the animals, leaving them tense and edgy.

She was thankful that the creatures were safe behind the wood-and-electric-wire fencing.

The bomb techs were working somewhere in the park, sweeping each building for explosives, but Maya was alone when she reached the pony ride area and shouted, "Hannah! Hannah, are you in here?"

Smothering the unease, she scanned the scene. Eight shaggy, child-sized ponies were tied to a railing near the entrance to a small sand-covered riding ring. Their eyes rolled white at the edges and their feet moved quickly, tapping up clouds of restive dust. She heard a low rumbling noise, like a plane flying overhead, though there was no sign of a contrail in the blue sky.

"Hannah?" she called again. "Your mother sent me to get you. Come on out, honey!"

But there was no sign of the child. *Check the pony rides,* the girl's mother had said, *she loves animals.*

Well, that hadn't panned out.

Maya reversed her direction and headed back toward Main Street. The girl couldn't have gone far. Maybe she'd wandered into the livery building to see the baby goats.

Or else she didn't wander at all, instinct whispered. The Mastermind had kidnapped children before and used them to draw Bear Claw officers into danger. The entire bomb squad was in the theme park. The chief and the others were nearby.

A big detonation would wipe out a big chunk of the task force.

Maya nearly spun and ran, nearly shouted for Sawyer to get his people out of the park. The only thing stopping her was the look she'd seen in the eyes of the other cops when her watch had run down and nothing happened. The look of disbelief.

They thought she'd called in a false alarm, just as they thought she was wrong about Henkes. If she evacuated the park again and nothing happened, her credibility would be shot once and for all. Did she dare run that risk?

Did she dare chance the alternative?

Maya swallowed hard and called, "Hannah?" one last time, thinking it futile.

Then she heard a small voice call, "Mommy?"

Relief spiked and Maya zeroed in on the livery building. The airplane noise increased as she bolted into the building and stumbled to a halt at the sight of a small girl, maybe six or seven years old, strapped upright to one of the leaning columns.

The dark-haired child was wearing a pink shirt and denim shorts, with sandals on her feet and tears streaming down her face. Her lips trembled when she saw Maya and she quavered, "I want my mommy!"

She struggled against her bonds, flailing with her feet and head, but making no progress against the thick leather strap that had been lashed across her chest and buckled on the other side of the pillar.

"Hold on, Hannah, I've got you!" Heart pounding, Maya crouched down beside the girl and went to work on her bonds, cursing the bastard who used innocents in his sick games. "Are you hurt?"

"N-no." The girl's voice cracked on the word and fresh tears streamed. "The ranch man told me—"

"We'll talk about it later," Maya said as she yanked the buckle free and hurled the leather strap to one side. She wanted to hear about this "ranch man," wanted to know if he looked like Henkes or one of his associates, but first things were first. "Come on, we've got to get out of there."

The airplane noise increased to a ground-shaking roar, only it didn't sound like an airplane anymore. It sounded more like...

Hoofbeats, Maya thought with a clarity born of terror.

The goats and sheep inside the petting zoo galloped in circles, becoming a bleating, milling mix of hooves and bodies. The lone bison in the far corner stomped, shook his head and reared partway up, as though he might jump out of his enclosure at any moment.

Maya's heart rabbited in her chest. "Come on!" She scooped the girl up and ran for the entrance, staggering beneath the weight of the child.

They were twenty feet from the door when a splintering crash sounded over the mind-blowing rumble that went on and on and on. Maya risked a look back, and nearly tripped and fell at what she saw.

Bison. Five, maybe ten of them, had broken through the back wall of the livery and were bearing down on her at a full-out gallop. Their small eyes were wide and scared, their nostrils flared with deep, sucking breaths, and their stubby horns cut the air as they charged. The penned animal bellowed and crashed through his fenced enclosure to join the others.

Maya turned and ran for her life.

Hannah's arms were wrapped around her neck in a chokehold that nearly cut off her breath, but Maya didn't care. She had to get the girl to safety. Had to get *herself* to safety.

But where was safe?

She burst through the petting zoo doors

and skidded onto the main road. Thinking that the bison would follow the path of least resistance, she bolted for the ticketing area, hoping the buildings and the turnstiles would deflect them. She could jump over while the bison turned, like some mad reenactment of the running of the bulls.

She heard shouts and gunshots, saw figures running along the ridges on either side of the ranch, and felt the growing hoof-beats in the trembling of the ground.

But the noise wasn't coming from behind her anymore. It was in front of her.

Suddenly, dust gouted from beyond the snack bar, which was the last building in line before the ticketing area. The noise increased to unbelievable proportions, as though Maya was caught in a tunnel with trains bearing down on her from either side.

She ran for the turnstiles, legs weak, lungs burning, too aware of the dozen bison bearing down on her from behind.

Then the dust in front of her thickened to shadows. Legs. Horns. Mad, panicked eyes. Twenty bison burst around the corner and turned down Main Street. Forty more followed them. A hundred. A full, panicked

stampede of thousand-pound animals gal-
loping hell-bent—

Directly at Maya and the little girl.

Chapter Three

Heart pounding a panicked rhythm in her ears, Maya bolted across the street, toward the snack bar, which had an ice cream booth on the flat-topped roof. She tightened her grip on Hannah and fixed her eyes on the stairs leading up to the snack area. Up. If she could just get up, she would be—

A heavy, hairy weight slammed into her from behind, driving her to her knees. Hooves struck her in the side and she curled her body around Hannah in a futile effort to protect the girl.

Then the pain and the blows were gone. Too quick, Maya thought. That couldn't have been the whole herd.

It wasn't, she realized moments later when she uncurled and looked around. She'd been struck by the offshoot group, the dozen animals who had burst through the livery after her. They had turned and galloped down Main Street.

The ground shook as the main herd bore down on her, no more than a city block away. The noise increased by the moment, hoof-beats overlaid with snorts and bellows and the sound of gunfire.

Maya saw white-rimmed eyes, red-flared nostrils and pounding, pulverizing hooves coming closer. Too close.

Knowing she was too late, that there was no way she was going to make it, Maya dragged herself to her feet, hauled the girl onto her hip and took two stumbling steps toward the stairs, toward safety. Her knee sang with pain. Her legs folded beneath her—

And strong arms grabbed her, lifted her and half carried her across the road as the air thickened with dust and fear.

Rough hands shoved her toward the stairs and a man's voice shouted, "Climb, damn it!"

Disbelieving, heart pounding, Maya climbed, aware of being crowded, being hustled, being shielded as her feet hit the stairs. She stumbled, needing both arms to hold the girl, and felt strong hands grab her waist and boost her upwards.

The leading edge of the stampede hit them. A big male bison demolished the lower stairs, blasting through the two-by-four construction as though it was made of matchsticks.

With nothing holding them off the ground, the upper stairs sagged and began to fall.

"Go!" Maya's rescuer shouted. He nearly threw her up over the edge, onto the low roof of the building. Wood splintered and Maya screamed as the stairs peeled away from the building to fall into the sea of hairy bodies below.

Carrying the man with them.

She pulled Hannah's arms from around her neck, set the girl on a safe spot well back from the edge and yelled, "Don't move!" Then she scrambled back to the place where the stairs had been, lay flat on her belly and poked her head over the precipice.

She saw a hand. A forearm. The top of a man's head. Her rescuer was clinging to the edge of the building as the herd passed below in a deadly thunder of hooves and horns.

"Hang on!" Maya lunged forward and

grabbed his arms; his shirt, anything she could get hold of to help him up and over.

His muscles were hard beneath her hands, his body powerful as he dragged himself over the edge and flopped down beside her, breathing heavily, one forearm thrown across his eyes.

"You okay?" he asked, voice ragged.

She took stock. Her body sang with the ache of bruises but not breaks, and when she glanced at Hannah, she saw that the girl was crying softly but appeared otherwise unhurt.

As the rumble of the stampede faded and human shouts and whistles took over, Maya cleared her throat of the hot, choking dust and the knowledge that without his help, she would have died. She swallowed hard and said, "We're okay. I can't thank you enough…" She trailed off, wanting a name for the stranger.

"Don't thank me. Let's just say this makes us even, okay?" He dragged his arm off his face, sat up and turned toward her.

Without the sunglasses, his eyes were two different shades of hazel, one so light as to border on amber, the other darkening to green, giving his face a skewness that should have been lopsided but instead was arresting. Interesting.

Familiar.

"Thorne!" she gasped, voice sharp with shock and memory.

For an instant, she was back in the High Top Bluff Police Academy. She'd seen him across the cafeteria, where he'd stood out from the others because he'd kept his long, sandy hair tied back in a ponytail, and wore a burnished gold, almost auburn five o'clock shadow at ten in the morning. He'd carried a casual air that was part poet, part surfer dude, and was the center of a growing throng. Maya later learned that people flocked to him, wanting to be included in the friendly, whiskey-laced charm that hid deeper things.

Darker things.

A murmur had run through the room, quick snatches of whispered rumor. *He was out in the field...undercover with Mason Falk's mountain men...captured...tortured...the drugs made him a little nuts...he's teaching psych while he heals...*

Uncomfortable with the sudden buzz, with the intimacy of knowing things about a complete stranger, Maya had gathered her things to leave, but when she passed the growing group, she'd glanced over at the man and found him watching her, found him nearer than she'd expected.

She had paused a moment, struck by the strangeness of his eyes, by the pull of him, by the click of recognition. No, she had never met him before, but she'd immediately recognized something about him. Something inside him, something deeper than the faint tang of alcohol that laced the air between them, though that, too, was a connection.

With the bruises of her marriage still fresh on her soul, Maya had pushed past the man, and had hidden in the back of his criminal psych class. He'd taught with an uncomfortable sort of detachment, as though he didn't want to be there, couldn't be anywhere else. More whispers had buzzed about him, rumors that he'd once identified a murderer by touching the victim's hand, that he had visions.

That he drank to keep the visions away.

Maya had stayed away from him, wary of the reputation and the alcohol, but every now and then, when they had come face to face in the halls, or on the jog paths, or in the cafeteria, he would look at her, and those strange, knowing eyes would linger in her mind for days.

That had been the only contact between them, the only connection until that one stupid, stupid night, when Maya had given in to the temptation.

As much as she'd told herself, then and now, that it was her fault more than his, that mistakes happened, that sometimes even the strongest person stumbled off the path, she'd lost something that night, something more than the six charms she'd plucked off her necklace the next morning, and flushed down the toilet.

She'd lost a piece of herself.

She felt the same strength drain from her as quickly as the blood drained from her face when she saw those eyes, when his features realigned themselves into those of the man she had known. His beard was gone and his hair cut short, and he was leaner now, fitter.

But he was still Thorne.

She thought she caught a whiff of alcohol on the air between them, though that could have been a scent memory, kicked up by the shock of seeing him again, the shock of the bison stampede that had nearly killed her.

His face creased into a wry smile. "We don't need to pretend this is a happy reunion. We don't need to rehash why you took off before I even woke up that morning, and why you transferred all the way out of the academy to avoid me afterward. Frankly, I don't think I care anymore. Just suffice it to say I owed you a good deed. Now we're even. Okay?"

He rose gracefully to his feet and extended a hand to her, though she wasn't sure whether he intended the gesture as a peace offering or a challenge.

Hell, she wasn't even sure which was appropriate.

What would he do if she admitted she didn't remember anything about that night? That everything after finding the dead battery on her car was a blur, culminating in her waking up the next morning in his bed, with his arm thrown across her waist and his breath in her ear?

"Fine." She stood on her own, strangely reluctant to touch him when her fingers still buzzed with the feel of his body as she'd helped pull him to safety. "We're even."

But her stomach twisted at the look in his eyes, which implied an uncomfortable intimacy. For years she'd tried to block the memory of her single ignominious one-night stand, tried to tell herself that nothing had happened, that he'd been gentleman enough not to take advantage. His expression now told her she'd been lying to herself about him, about them.

They'd gotten drunk, they'd had sex, and then she'd run away.

Emotions she'd fought off five years earlier rose up to swamp her, to slap at her with feelings of failure, of humiliation, of disappointment—not with him, but with herself.

She drew breath to say something breezy, something that belied the turmoil within, but before she could speak, a small voice said, "I want my mommy."

Startled back to the moment, to the case, Maya looked over at Hannah, who sat nearby with tears drying on her face.

Thorne crouched down near the girl. "And who is this?"

"She's Hannah," Maya answered. She bent down, picked up the girl—thankful that she was small for her age—and balanced the child on her hip, needing the contact perhaps more than Hannah did. "And she'll need to spend some time with Alissa."

Thorne's strange eyes sharpened. "Why?"

Maya took a breath and tried to figure out how to summarize the situation without upsetting the traumatized girl further. "Let's just say she wasn't in the petting zoo by accident. She had help getting there, and my guess is that she was intended to draw more cops into the park before the stampede." She paused and fussed with Hannah's shirt so she wouldn't have to look at Thorne. "I assume you're on loan for the Master—" She broke off as the obvious conclusion clicked in her brain.

Oh, hell.

She spun and glared at him, as anger, frustration and a strange sort of betrayal flooded her system. "Tell me you're not my replacement."

BUT HE DIDN'T TELL HER that. He couldn't. Instead, Thorne looked away, down to where a half dozen mounted ranch hands were driving the exhausted bison into a far pasture, while cops crawled over a section of downed fence, no doubt looking for clues that the stampede had been rigged.

When he spoke, his voice was low. "It's only a temporary thing."

She narrowed her eyes, making him wonder what she saw in him, what she was thinking. But she merely said, "Seriously? You're just here to fill in until Internal Affairs clears me to get my badge back?"

"I'm here to help bring down the bastard who set you up today," Thorne said. He hadn't answered her question, but the chief had urged him to keep quiet about the possibility of taking over the psych specialist's role in the Bear Claw Forensics Department. The evasion burned, letting him know that even though he'd saved her life, he still owed her.

Because the irony was that she'd saved his life five years earlier, and she didn't even know it.

He jammed his hands in his pockets. "Look, Maya. I—"

"You two okay up there?" a voice shouted from below. The top rungs of an aluminum extension ladder banged against the lip of the roof, and shook with ascending footsteps.

"We're fine," Thorne yelled back, louder

than he'd meant to. He glanced at Maya. "Let's talk about it later."

Her eyes grew wary, her expression shuttered. "There's no need."

Maya's friends were the first two up the ladder. Alissa and Cassie shot Thorne nearly identical looks of distrust, then rushed to assure themselves that Maya was fine. Homicide detective Tucker McDermott was next to gain the roof. After speaking with Maya for a moment, he took Hannah and carried her down the ladder.

Moments later, the sounds of a tearful mother-daughter reunion rose up from below.

"The chief wants to see you back at the PD," Cassie told Maya. She had her back to Thorne, but her words carried.

Aware that their conversation remained unfinished, that their reunion had none of the joyful ring of Hannah's return to her mother, Thorne stepped forward. "I'll drive her. We have things to discuss."

Maya didn't make eye contact when she said, "I've got my own wheels. I'll drive myself."

Realizing that he was the one without the

wheels, Thorne grimaced. "Then I'll ride with you. I came in with the chief."

"Then you can leave with him, too," Cassie said. She stepped forward, leading with her chin as though daring him to throw a punch. "Isn't it enough that you're using her desk and you've got all her notes on the Mastermind case?"

Maya surprised him by stepping forward and laying a hand on her friend's arm. "I've got it." She gestured toward the ladder. "You two head down. I'll be there in a minute."

When Thorne and Maya were alone again on the roof, she turned to face him, arms folded across her chest. As though remembering his old lectures on open versus closed body language, she uncrossed her arms and hooked her thumbs in the waistband of her jeans, where a narrow green belt glittered with a faint gold pattern. "Look," she began, "I don't know how much Chief Parry told you about what's going on, but I'll be back on the job as soon as IA clears me."

"Of course," Thorne agreed, though he noticed that she was still avoiding eye contact, and her fingers worked restlessly at her sides. She wasn't as confident as she seemed. He felt a slash of empathy as he remembered his own down time following his escape from Mason Falk's compound. He'd been on medical leave for nearly six months, and sent to teach at the Academy in High Top Bluff for a year after that.

He'd worked his way back into active duty. Maya would do the same, if she wanted it enough. But based on what the chief had told him, it didn't seem likely that she would return to the Bear Claw PD. If that was a given, was there really any harm in him angling for her job?

Thorne wasn't sure yet. He hadn't fully processed the fact that this was Maya Cooper. Pretty, shy Maya Cooper from the back row of his psych class, who never raised her hand, but who aced all the quizzes and papers.

Pretty Maya Cooper who had cried in his arms over the whiskey he'd urged on her, making him step back and realize what he was becoming.

What he had already become.

He might not have changed his life because of her, but he'd damn well changed it because of what she'd shown him about himself. That meant he owed her, but how much?

"Let me ride with you," he urged, not completely sure why he wanted to spend time with her. "Even if it's only temporary, I'm here to work the Mastermind case. I'd appreciate your insights."

She looked at him for a long moment, as though judging his motives, or maybe his sincerity. Apparently she found one or both lacking, because she shook her head. "Read my notes. They're organized and complete, such as they are. You want a hint? Have Hannah describe the guy who grabbed her, and let Alissa develop a sketch." She shrugged. "Beyond that, you're on your own."

"Come on, Maya." He took a step closer to her, then paused at the unfamiliar rev that sped through his body. Acknowledging the danger signal, he cleared his throat and said, "Help me out, here. We're on the same team."

"Funny that you should mention teams," she said, expression closed. "I seem to remember that you were a player and a partier. Unfortunately for you, I'm not either of those things anymore." A measure of tension left her shoulders, as though she'd needed to say that aloud. "Look," she said in a less brittle tone, "if I thought I knew anything that isn't in my notes, I'd tell you. But it's all there, everything right up until I was suspended."

"And what about since then?" he asked quietly. "I'll bet you've done some snooping on your own."

"Why do you care?" she snapped. "You don't need me on this case. There's no reason for us to spend time together." She pursed her lips, which were fuller than he remembered. "You're not thinking that you and I are going to take up where we left off, are you?"

"No," he said too quickly. "God, no!" He held up a hand. "No offense or anything, but I just got out of a relationship," such as it was, "and it didn't end well. She was a coworker, and—" And he was talking too much. Maya didn't need to know the sordid details of Detective Tabitha Stock and her personal agenda. He frowned and ended with, "Let's just say we can put the past in the past and keep it there. I'm not looking for anything more than your take on the Mastermind case."

"Then read my notes." She turned away and slipped over the side of the building, down the ladder and was gone, leaving Thorne alone on the roof.

But her presence lingered in the air, in the hum of blood through his body, the buzz that said she was prettier than he remembered, spunkier than he remembered. But beneath that buzz was a wariness, a recognition that she'd grown into a dedicated, driven cop, the kind of cop who'd do anything to protect her territory, to ensure her job and move her career forward. Just like Tabitha.

Maya wasn't his problem. She didn't want his help or company, and he'd made things square by pulling her away from the stampeding bison. He could move on from here, without giving her another thought.

Moments later, he cursed, climbed down the ladder and set off after her. The bomb threat and the Mastermind's previous pattern of going after women in the Forensics Department suggested she was a target, which made her his problem.

What better way to find the Mastermind than to stick close to his next victim?

THE MASTERMIND WATCHED THE cops disperse to their vehicles and hid a smirk at the thought that everything was going according to plan. They were stirred up now, anxious and ready to jump at the smallest shadow.

He would wait a day, maybe longer, until the anticipation had built to a fever pitch. Then he would make his next move.

He picked out the slight figure of a dark-haired woman, identifying her by the aggressive wiggle of her hips as she walked to her car. The taller, stronger figure of a man followed at a distance.

"Right on schedule," he murmured. He was particularly proud of this facet of his plan.

Though the ability to manipulate people wasn't one he'd intentionally cultivated, it had served him well. With a few minor—and fixable—hiccups, everything was moving smoothly. The Bear Claw cops were formidable adversaries, but that would only make his inevitable victory that much sweeter when it came.

Smiling now, he turned away and headed toward his vehicle. He had a few matters to attend to, new preparations for the next stage of events.

Then he had a phone call to make.

Chapter Four

Maya wasn't surprised that Thorne snagged
a cruiser and followed her to the BCCPD
rather than staying at the ranch with the
evidence techs. What surprised her was how
quickly she noticed, and how thoroughly
he'd invaded her thoughts.

As she drove through the early afternoon
Bear Claw traffic, her back ached with hoof
print–shaped sore spots and her legs shook
with reaction to the stampede. Frustrated im-
potence pounded through her at the knowledge that the Mastermind was back on the
attack and she was off the force.

But those emotions were layered beneath
baffled confusion and brown-tinted memories. She hadn't expected to see Thorne Coleridge ever again. She hadn't kept tabs on him,

hadn't wanted to know where he was or what he was doing.

She'd wanted to forget everything about him, everything about that night. Hell, she'd transferred right out of the High Top Bluff Academy to avoid dealing with what had happened.

It had been the smartest move she'd ever made, because she'd transferred into the Boulder Academy, where she'd met Cassie and Alissa. But end results aside, she'd been running and she damn well knew it. Running from herself, not him. But now that he was back in her life, she would have to deal with—

"Nothing," she said aloud as she pulled into the PD parking lot and felt a spurt of dismay to see an unfamiliar car in her usual parking spot, emphasizing that this wasn't her territory anymore. She swallowed and gave herself a pep talk. "You don't have to see him, don't have to talk to him, don't have to do anything with him. He's got your notes and you're off the case. It's not your responsibility anymore."

But the words rang false, banging up against the vow she'd made just that morning, when she'd decided it was time to stop sulking because nobody believed her, time to get out there and prove that her Wexton Henkes was their man. Their Mastermind.

"To hell with it," she said, though she wasn't sure whether she was rejecting Thorne, her vow or the whole complicated mess. She climbed out of the car and stalked into the PD, ignoring the stab of nostalgia for the walk she'd taken almost daily for the first nine months she'd lived in Bear Claw, and had managed only a handful of times in the past three months, while her suspension dragged on.

She had taken two steps toward the conference room when Chief Parry appeared in his office doorway. "We'll meet in here."

Maya paused. "But the task force meetings are always in the conference—" Then she stopped herself, took a breath and nodded. "Of course. Sorry."

Aware of the curious stares of the desk clerks and the cops gathered outside the conference room, she lifted her chin, not wanting them to know how much it bothered her to be back in the PD with no resolution of her status in sight. She held her back stiff as she strode into the chief's office and sat in the visitor's chair, feeling every inch an intruder in her own workplace.

Chief Parry remained standing in the doorway, and moments later called, "There you are, Coleridge. I want you in here, too."

Maya winced but didn't protest. What would be the use? Instead, she schooled her expression to professional blankness as Thorne entered the room and the chief closed the door before taking the chair behind his wide, cluttered desk. In the absence of a third chair, Thorne leaned back against the glass door and shoved his hands in his pockets in a study of casual interest.

His presence filled the room and scraped her already raw nerve endings, but she didn't let it show. Instead, she turned her back on Thorne and focused on the chief. "You wanted to see me, sir?"

Parry sat silent for a moment, and his eyes flicked to Thorne and back to her, passing a silent message she couldn't interpret, one that set her nerves to a razor's edge. Then the chief said, "Look, Cooper, I know this hasn't been easy for you, but you're not helping yourself one bit with these antics."

A nasty disquiet twisted in her stomach. "I'm not sure I'm following you."

The chief scowled. "What were you doing at the Chuckwagon Ranch?"

Knowing he was going to be ticked, Maya shifted in her chair. "When I was checking on connections between the State Park and the Natural History Museum, I found that Wexton Henkes is on both boards. Turns out he's also a major underwriter of the college hockey rink and owns most of the Chuckwagon Ranch." She paused, aware that the chief's face was rapidly purpling. "I thought I'd check the place out for myself."

"And nearly got yourself killed, along with an innocent child," Thorne said. His voice was quiet, but loaded with condemnation. "You didn't think to bring this to Chief Parry? To your friends in the Forensics Department? You thought going Lone Ranger was a good idea? What if you'd gotten yourself—"

"It was a fishing expedition," she interrupted without turning toward him. "I never expected Henkes to come after me like that. If I had just—"

"Enough!" Parry slapped his desk hard

enough to make the papers jump. "I've had enough of you persecuting Henkes. First the child abuse thing and now this? I won't hear of it." He made a short, vicious chopping motion with his hand. "It's over, do you hear me? We both know you haven't got any evidence. You've got theories and your own personal bias. I don't know what you've got against Henkes and frankly, I don't care. I just want you to leave him alone. Hell, I want you to leave the case alone." He fixed her with a look. "That's an order."

And if I disobey? Maya almost asked. If she wasn't on the force—at least temporarily—then he couldn't give her orders, could he?

But the *temporarily* part was the sticking point, she knew. If she wanted her job back, she'd have to play along.

As though he'd guessed her thoughts, the chief scowled. "Don't cross me on this one, Cooper. Not unless you want the IA investigation to drag on indefinitely." He waited a beat as though he expected her to argue. When she didn't, his expression relaxed. "Fine. As long as we're clear on that." He waved her out. "That's all."

Thorne eased away from the door and pushed it open for her, but when he moved to follow, the chief called him back. As the glass panel closed at Maya's back, she found twenty faces staring at her with expressions ranging from curiosity to distrust. She glared back, telling herself to show a strong front, but inside she was cringing.

How had it come to this? She had moved to Bear Claw full of excitement about starting a new life, a new department with her friends, working under a police chief who had the reputation of being tough but fair. Now look at her—suspended, distrusted, disgusted...

She nearly let out a whimper. She wanted to escape to the basement, to the quiet corner of the downstairs office where she kept her desk and her things.

Only it wasn't her desk anymore. For the time being, it was Thorne's.

And later? Who knew.

So she turned for the back exit, only to hear the door open and the chief's voice say, "Cooper!"

She turned, feeling the sting of not being "Officer" anymore. "Yes?"

Parry's expression was blank, his voice carried across the room when he said, "Wait by the door. I'll have an officer escort you home. Until further notice, I want you to take all possible precautions. The bomb threat and the stampede indicate that our Mastermind has targeted you."

He could have said any of that in private. That he'd chosen to broadcast the information across the packed main room, meant one of two things in Maya's book. Either he wanted to warn the other officers to look out for her, or he'd meant to remind them that she was a civilian.

She had to assume the latter.

Feeling the familiar mix of anger and frustration that had dogged her ever since she woke up in a hospital bed with no memory of attacking Henkes, Maya spun for the door. She wanted to push straight through, but she waited as ordered.

She wasn't an idiot. She knew what the incidents at the ranch meant. She'd been targeted by a killer, just as Cassie and Alissa had been before her.

Only the difference was that she knew who was after her.

Wexton Henkes. Philanthropist. Child abuser.

Their Mastermind. She was sure of it. But how could she convince the others?

"Come on," Thorne's voice said behind her, startling her. "I'll follow you." He didn't wait for her, instead pushing past, out of the PD toward the parking lot.

Maya followed slowly. "Shouldn't you sit in on the task force meeting?"

"The chief will fill me in later."

As she climbed into her hatchback and started the engine, Maya tried not to let it bother her that the other cops were filing into the conference room at that very moment. Cassie would sit in the corner of the room where the three of them had always sat, alone most likely, because Alissa would be downstairs working with the little girl, Hannah, trying to develop a sketch of the ranch man who'd taken her from her mother and restrained her in the petting zoo as bait.

But bait for whom? Maya wondered as she pulled out of the PD, aware of Thorne following too close behind. The Mastermind would have no reason to assume she would go after the child—any of the other cops would have done the same. So it stood to reason that the phone call had been aimed at her, but the stampede had been targeted at the Bear Claw cops in general.

But to what end?

After a short drive, Maya pulled into the underground garage beneath the ultra-modern building in the heart of downtown Bear Claw that she called home. She'd bought the condo with the last of the settlement money she'd received in her long-ago divorce, and considered the two-bedroom, split-level home way better than Dane Arkent's memory deserved.

Then again, she hadn't been worth much back then, either. She'd been young and stupid when she married Dane. She'd been a hard partier who'd fought constantly with her conservative parents and had seen the older man, a professional journalist, as her ticket out of small-town boredom. The fact that he'd partied just as hard, if not harder, was a bonus. Or maybe it had been the attraction, she wasn't sure anymore.

Hell, it didn't matter now. She'd gotten out of the relationship, and she'd made herself into a better, stronger person.

Or so she told herself. But the words rang

faintly false when Thorne's bootfalls echoed against the cement of the parking garage and her heart skittered, skipping a beat in her chest at the sight of his wide shoulders and the lean lethality of his body.

He had been an angry, banged-up cop with a layer of whiskey flab when she'd known him before.

Now, wearing a shoulder holster he must have donned in the car, he looked every inch the lean, deadly warrior. But as Maya felt a traitorous quiver of warmth in her midsection, she reminded herself that looks could be deceiving. Just because he'd changed on the outside didn't mean he'd changed his basic personality, his basic drives. Everything she'd seen of him so far—from the expensive clothes and the snazzy shades to the faint hint of danger he wore like a cloak—indicated he was the same Thorne she'd known in High Top Bluff.

The same Thorne she'd run from because she'd needed to pull herself back together and knew damn sure she wouldn't manage it if he were near, acting as the human embodiment of her temptation.

She held up a hand when he drew near.

"Thanks for following me, but you don't have to come up. The doors are key-coded."

"The Mastermind—whoever he is—has already proven himself smart enough to tap dance around key codes," Thorne said bluntly. "I'm coming up."

"Suit yourself." Maya tried to keep the resentment out of her voice, but those three words—*whoever he is*—said it as clear as day. Thorne didn't believe that Wexton Henkes could be the Mastermind. The chief hadn't believed it either. Hell, nobody in Bear Claw wanted to believe the worst of Henkes. They wanted to see the philanthropist. The soon-to-be congressman.

They didn't want to see what she saw.

The elevator ride was uncomfortable. The small space was too warm, as though the air conditioners were off. Colorado was far cooler than South Carolina, where her parents had tried to raise her with Sunday School and strictness, but there was still enough summer heat to prickle a fine film of sweat on the back of her neck, beneath her suddenly heavy-feeling hair.

"This way," she said, gesturing unnecessarily to one of the two doors off the elevator lobby on the fifth floor, her floor. Her tongue felt glued to the roof of her mouth, as though she'd invited him home for another, more intimate purpose than checking her closets for an intruder.

She fumbled for the lock, got it open on the second try, and let him through first. He pulled his service piece out of the shoulder holster and slipped the safety off. Instead of reassuring her, the sight of the weapon brought a sting of resentment.

One of the detectives had collected her gun as evidence, and the chief had suspended her permit to carry along with her badge.

He'd left her defenseless, then sent Thorne to protect her. There was a certain irony to that. Maya figured she might even find it amusing in a few months, once the Mastermind was caught, IA cleared her to return to the force and Thorne went back to wherever he'd come from.

In other words, once life was back to normal.

Thorne prowled the first floor, from the kitchen to the sitting area and the bath, then up the stairs to her master bedroom, office and spare room. She tried to remember whether she'd made the bed that morning, then told herself it didn't matter worth a damn. She wasn't trying to impress anyone.

"All clear," he reported minutes later as he descended the stairs, reholstering his weapon as he walked.

"You should get back to the meeting, then." She held the door open in invitation, but he stood his ground, measuring her with his mismatched eyes.

"I'd like to get your input on this," he said finally. "Your notes tell me that you've got insight into this guy, and what happened today proves that he's set his sights on you."

She frowned, immediately on the defensive. "Why the turnaround? Not twenty minutes ago, the chief ordered me to stay the hell away from the case. Now you're inviting me back on? It doesn't wash."

Besides, as much as she wanted to be back in, as much as she longed for the teamwork and the sense of belonging, she didn't want to work with Thorne.

That would be a bad idea. A really, really bad idea.

"I'm not asking you to be a formal member of the team, or even a civilian consultant," Thorne said slowly, as though he was testing out the concept for himself. "However, I'd like to be kept in the loop if you're going off on your own, and I'd like the opportunity to run things by you when I have a question."

But he wouldn't meet her eyes, and his tense shoulders and jaw screamed of reluctance. He didn't want to work with her. Ergo, he'd been ordered to extend the offer, and it didn't take a genius to figure who or why.

Chief Parry wanted someone to babysit her.

Thorne was under orders to keep her away from the Henkes case. She'd bet on it.

Maya crossed her arms tighter, wishing she could tell Thorne to go to hell. But common sense wouldn't let her. In reality, this might be her only chance to get back into the game, and she might even be able to convince him to listen to her theories.

Whatever she and Thorne had—or hadn't— shared, he was an outsider in Bear Claw, just like her. They weren't bound by Henkes's politics or popularity. Maybe, just maybe she could get him on her side.

She didn't want to work with him, didn't want to be near him and feel the shameful memories or the burn of an attraction she'd thought had died years ago. Didn't want to risk the temptation, or the possibility of sliding back into old, destructive patterns. But at the same time, she'd be damned if she let the Mastermind take more innocent lives, damned if she let him drop another cloak of fear across Bear Claw City.

Was her own comfort level more important than the innocents she was sworn to protect?

Of course not.

"Okay." Maya uncrossed her arms and hooked her thumbs over her green lizard belt. "But on one condition."

Thorne regarded her, eyes unreadable. "Which is?"

"You give me the opportunity to present my case against Wexton Henkes. You have to listen, really listen without any of the preconceived notions the chief and the other locals bring to the table."

"And if I don't buy into your theory?"

Maya felt a spurt of relief, of victory laced with the knowledge that she was riding the fine edge between success and disaster. "We'll cope with that if and when it happens. Do we have a deal?"

She held out her hand to shake on it, only then realizing the foolishness of the move. But before she could pull back, he said, "Yes, we've got a deal," and took her hand.

The touch of palm to palm was electric. Powerful. More damaging than it ought to have been. His eyes darkened, the mismatched pupils widening until there was more black than hazel, until they seemed to look straight into her.

Her heart lodged in her throat, and for a mad, crazy minute she wondered what he saw.

Wondered how many of the stories about him were true.

But before she could ask, he pulled away and strode to the door, expression shuttered. "Bolt the door behind me. I'll pick you up tomorrow morning and we can get started."

And then he was gone. His presence echoed in the air, on her skin, in the beat of her heart. The neat condo seemed suddenly empty, though her brain teemed with reawakened memories of the High Top Bluff Academy, where the female students had followed Thorne with their eyes, then whispered when he was past.

She set the lock and chain with numb fingers, though she told herself she had nothing to fear in her own home. Almost without conscious thought, she crossed the living room and passed into the kitchen, which was separated from the rest of the open first floor by a waist-high breakfast bar topped with green, blue and orange mosaic tiling. Cabinets lined the other three sides of the small area, some beginning at the parquet, others hanging above the yellow tiled countertop. She opened the first of them and pulled out a glass bottle most of the way filled with a lovely clear liquid.

She touched the bottle to her cheek and rolled the label across her lips.

The bottle was an old friend. Eleven years she'd had it. Eleven years it had gone unopened in her cabinet, set front and center like a sentinel. A symbol.

But not anymore. Now the seal was broken, had been for months.

She set the bottle on the breakfast bar and dropped into one of the stools, so she could fold her arms on the tile mosaic, press her cheek to her folded hands, and stare at the label, where a handsome man stood in the full warrior's regalia of another time. His sandy hair was long and his muscles bulged across his chest and calves. His eyes were shaded beneath the brim of a flipped-up faceplate, but now, as always before, she swore he winked at her through mismatched eyes.

Want kindled hard and hot in her belly, the want of a man, of a drink. Of oblivion.

The phone rang.

Maya screeched and jumped, shoving back from the breakfast bar and nearly tipping the stool in her haste as she saw the bottle and realized what she'd nearly done.

She grabbed the phone automatically, and licked her suddenly parched lips. "Hello?"

"I saw you climb up on the roof with him."

The computer-modulated voice sent a sharp, ferocious slice of cold through her midsection, where it tangled with the sick roil of temptation. She tightened her fingers on the phone. "How did you get this number?"

"That's not the right question," the voice said, and tsked with disappointment. "I'll only answer the right question."

"What is the right question?" she asked, heart pounding into her throat as she tried to find her psych specialist's calm where there was no peace to be had.

"Not that one," he said, and for a moment she thought he'd hung up. But then his voice said, "I saw him at your place this evening, too. Handsome fellow. It's really too bad."

She cursed herself for playing along when she asked, "What's too bad?"

"Look outside your window," the voice said.

And the line went dead.

Chapter Five

Thorne jingled his keys in his hand as he crossed the underground garage, the noise providing a metallic counterpoint to his footsteps. His personal ride—a decommissioned police Interceptor that was neither cool nor sexy, but that went like a bat out of hell and never quit on him—sat where he'd parked it, looking undisturbed.

His gut tightened and a spurt of adrenaline warned him that all was not well, but he couldn't see a damn thing wrong with the car.

"It's the woman," he said aloud. "She's what's wrong."

Or more accurately, his response to her was a problem. An unacceptable complication. It was bad enough he felt the gut-punch of attraction to a woman he was looking to beat out of a job. Worse were the flashes he'd gotten the two times they'd touched—once at the ranch and once again just now, when they'd shaken on the "deal" Chief Parry had ordered him to offer.

He didn't want to babysit a suspended cop while he worked on a case the Bear Claw force hadn't managed to put to rest in nearly nine months' worth of full-time task force effort. And he sure as hell didn't want to babysit this particular cop. Not when touching her triggered the moments of pre-science he'd fought so hard to block.

It was ironic, really. She'd been the catalyst for him learning to block the visions. Now she was breaking down those hard-won barriers, and she didn't even know it.

Some of his so-called cop friends in Wagon Ridge—including Tabitha—had pressed him to tune in on the flashes, to use them to solve cases. They'd wanted to turn him into some sort of freaky psychic detective, a sideshow or a conversation piece. They hadn't understood that the visions weren't like on TV, where some poor schlub put his hands on a knife and instantly saw the perp's face in glowing Technicolor.

No, it was messier than that. More painful.

Less sure. Each flash reminded him of the days he'd spent captive in Mason Falk's mountain stronghold, reminded him of the drugs and the electric charges the cult leader had used to torture him. To break him. To force him to disclose how much the High Top Bluff PD knew about the cult's planned attack on the town.

He hadn't given up the names or dates, but he'd been broken nonetheless. His mind had been injured, his link between now and then had cracked, letting something else bleed through. Something that seemed like ESP, but felt like pain. Like death.

Like murder.

Thorne cursed and started the Interceptor, which responded with a double-throated roar of raw power. "Not again. I'm not going back there again."

He'd fought the flashes before. He could fight them again.

He gunned the engine and sent the dark green cruiser out of the parking garage with a chirp of heavy-duty, high-speed tires. The violence simmered just beneath the surface of his soul, sending a fine tracework of electricity along his skin. Images of death and destruction crackled at the edges of his mind, and he cursed as he swung the Interceptor out of the garage, onto the empty street. He hit the accelerator, needing to outrun the memories—

And a figure lunged from the building and hurtled in front of his car.

It was Maya, waving her hands and shouting.

"Damn it!" Thorne stomped the brake, and when that wasn't enough to stop the heavy vehicle in time, he twisted the wheel and sent the car behind her, up onto the sidewalk, then back down onto the road. The rear end shimmied and then cut loose in a vicious skid that had him cursing and fighting the wheel.

A delivery truck rounded the corner of the city block, taking up the lane he needed. Thorne saw the driver's face, saw that impact was inevitable.

He let the steering wheel spin through his fingers and braced for the crunch.

A nanosecond later, the Interceptor whipped back into the right lane and slid to a stop, barely bumping up against a navy blue mailbox as it came to rest, well clear of the delivery truck.

The engine stalled and Thorne's world went silent.

His heart didn't beat. His blood didn't flow. His chest didn't rise. There was absolute, chilling stillness in his head.

Like death.

Then everything came back at once. His heart rocketed in his ears and the delivery truck's air brakes released with a loud hiss as the guy drove on, maybe because he was on a tight schedule, maybe because he couldn't be bothered to help.

Or maybe because he saw that Thorne already had someone coming to his rescue.

Maya yanked open the door. "Are you okay?"

Her brown eyes were wide and scared, her fine-boned features pinched, as though she'd seen a ghost.

Or nearly created one.

"What the hell were you thinking?" Thorne bellowed. He yanked off his seat belt and lunged from the car so he could go toe-to-toe with her when he shouted, "I could have killed you! Hell, you could have killed me! What sort of idiotic stunt was that?"

It was then that he realized how physically

small she was. He topped her by nearly a
foot, and was probably double her weight.
Her stature was almost childlike, but there
was nothing immature about the fire in her
eyes, or the way the soft curves of her breasts
rose and fell as she breathed heavily and
scowled up at him.

"I'm not the idiot who was doing fifty on
a city street. What is *your* problem?"

"You have no idea," he replied cryptically,
and stepped back, creating a chasm of empty
space between them and bringing a sense of
coolness where there had been heat moments
before. He jammed his hands in his pockets.
"Why the hell are you down here jumping in
front of cars when I specifically told you to
lock yourself in the condo?"

He expected her to snap back that he
wasn't her keeper. So he was surprised when
her eyes darkened and some of the fight
drained out of her. Her voice sounded small
and scared when she said, "He called me
again. He said he'd seen you walk me to my
door, and that I should look out my window.
The way he said it, I knew something was
going to happen to you."

"But I'm not the target," Thorne said automatically, "you are." Inside him, the anger fought to get free, fought to rise at the thought that the bastard had called her again, had tried to touch her again, if only through his mechanically altered voice.

But did he? a voice whispered deep inside Thorne, the sly, suspicious voice he sometimes ignored, sometimes heeded.

He had seen the suspicion in some of the other officers' faces when they spoke of Maya. Or rather, when they didn't speak of her. They thought she had snapped and gone after Henkes. They wondered whether she'd faked the bomb threat that afternoon.

What if she had? What if she was fabricating this new call? His instincts stirred to life as what he remembered of her from before clashed with what he'd been told by the chief and others. He remembered her as a quiet, studious woman with shadows in the backs of her eyes and a wicked grin that didn't show nearly often enough.

It had been that grin that had pulled him in. It had been the tears that had kept him a gentleman. He had been attracted to her back then, and part of him still wanted her. That much hadn't changed.

What had changed?

"Maybe we've both been targeted." She crossed her arms and looked away. "You're part of the Forensics Department now, at least temporarily."

He winced internally at the catch in her voice, at the knowledge that she was banking on getting her job back. But aloud, he said, "That's true enough, but I wasn't in any danger until you jumped in front of my car and nearly got us both killed."

Her eyes flashed. "I know what I heard. He told me to look out my window. I thought—" She faltered, then continued, "I thought he'd rigged your car to explode. That I'd look down and watch you die."

The word *you* suddenly seemed too personal, as though she had worried for him as a man, not just in the abstract. As though she'd run downstairs and out into the street to save *him,* not just another cop.

Thorne shifted uncomfortably and glanced at the Interceptor, still parked up against the mailbox, diagonally across the right lane of traffic. "Get in. I'll park back in the garage and we can head upstairs. We'll call it in from there. No way I'm leaving you alone now."

Whether she'd received a call or not, something was going on here.

"I think we should head back to the station," she said quietly, then cut a glance at him. "We need to run the delivery van that nearly hit you. Didn't you think it was odd to see a ski outfitter's truck this time of year?"

"I was a little busy at the time. I didn't get the name on the van, or the plates." But Thorne thought back, picturing the driver's face the moment before their almost-impact.

Christ, she was right. The driver hadn't looked shocked or scared. He'd looked determined.

And he'd steered into Thorne's skid.

A slick chill worked its way into his gut. What if she was right? What if the driver had been aiming *for* him?

That would mean she'd been telling the truth.

And she'd saved his life. Again.

MAYA HELD IT TOGETHER UNTIL they got to the PD, but when the chief took one look at her and immediately glanced at Thorne for an explanation, the emotions closed in on her.

She turned away from the men as panic slammed against frustration, then took a backseat to anger.

She hadn't asked for any of this, damn it. All she'd ever wanted was to do her job and do it well. She'd wanted a chance to atone for her past mistakes.

Instead, it seemed like she was making more new ones each day.

Thorne's voice spoke suddenly from behind her. "If you want to wait downstairs, I'll call your desk when we're ready for you."

Surprised, Maya turned to him. She saw sympathy in his mismatched eyes, rather than the dark anger that had simmered between them during the brief ride to head-quarters.

She took a step back, unsettled by his nearness, by the hum of her emotions too close to the surface of her soul. Without another word, she strode to the stairs leading down to the basement. The crime lab had been remodeled nine months earlier when they'd first started work, and again during the Canyon Kidnapping case, when a bomb had detonated in the lab space, nearly killing Alissa and Tucker. Now, the three large rooms were divided into an expansive crime lab, plus two adjoining offices the women had streamlined to their individual needs.

Cassie's microscopes, DNA amplification units and fluorescent analysis machines were ranged alongside Alissa's state-of-the-art reconstruction equipment. Maya swallowed hard at the familiar hum of the equipment, at the sense of coming home.

She tried not to let her descent into familiar territory feel like a retreat.

The three interconnected rooms were dark, lit only by the occasional beacons of emergency lamps and equipment LED lights. The dimness reminded her that it was just past quitting time, though regular business hours meant little to the Bear Claw cops, especially those on the task force.

Cassie and Alissa must be out on the case. Maya felt a slice of disappointment that she'd missed her friends. But alongside that was a strong sense of relief that she had the place to herself. There was nobody around to see her shoulders slump as she walked into the smaller shared office, nobody to see her drop into the chair behind what had once been her desk.

Nobody to see her fold her arms atop a scattering of papers and drop her cheek onto them. Tears pressed, but she held them back and touched a fingertip to the charms she wore around her neck.

Five charms. Five years of successfully resisting temptation.

Now she was back to square one.

Or was she? What had really happened that night at Weston Henkes's mansion? Had she truly—

"You okay?"

Maya jolted upright at a touch on her shoulder, but bit back the squeak of alarm when she recognized the voice and the honey-blond hair pulled up under a BCCPD ball cap. "Alissa! What are you doing here?"

Her friend quirked a half smile. "I work here, remember?" Then she winced. "Sorry. That was mean."

"No," Maya countered, burying the unintended sting, "It's the truth. The real question is what am *I* doing here?"

Alissa hit the lights before she moved around the desk and sat in a visitor's chair, which hadn't been there when Maya had last used the office. That detail brought a pang, as did the subtle differences she noticed now that the room was fully illuminated. Her piles remained on the desk, but her computer had been shifted slightly, and the mouse was positioned on the left of the keyboard, not the right. Thorne had just arrived, which meant that someone else had used her space, touched her things.

She tried not to let it bother her.

"I heard he called you again," Alissa said without preamble, her eyes reflecting her worry. "I don't like that."

"I'm not exactly turning handsprings, either," Maya said. She'd aimed her tone for dry, but it came out sounding more plaintive than she'd intended.

"What happened?"

Knowing she would have to go over it again in a few minutes with Thorne and the chief, she quickly sketched out the phone call for her friend. She left out the physical sparks she'd sensed—or imagined—between her and Thorne in the elevator and in her apartment, but couldn't quite mask the fear she'd felt when she'd thought he was in danger.

It was concern for a fellow cop, she told

herself, but heard her voice hitch on the details and cursed herself for the weakness, for falling back toward the same pattern of mistakes when she damn well knew better.

Thorne was as much a temptation for her as the rum. She'd learned that once before, and didn't need to repeat the lesson.

When she got to the part about the delivery van, Alissa's eyes sharpened. "Did you get a look at the van and the driver?"

"Yes, but Thorne traced the license plate back to a stolen vehicle. I—" Maya broke off as she realized she was talking to a woman whose first and best love was sketching, though her talents had been underutilized within the Bear Claw PD. "Hell yes, I saw the driver!"

Alissa leaned over to her desk—which wasn't much of a stretch in the small office— and snagged a spiral-bound sketchpad and a cup full of pencils, some plain lead, some colored. "Was his face round or oval?"

Though the forensics department had sophisticated software packages capable of generating uncanny likenesses from witness descriptions, the programs worked on human averages rather than feel, and were limited by their templates. Alissa preferred sketching the old-fashioned way when possible, and had a damn good record doing it her way.

Maya closed her eyes and tried to picture the scene out in front of her building. She edited out the emotions and focused on the van.

"He had an oval face," she said, trying to put the image into words, "but his jaw was square. More like a bottom-heavy oval." She described the driver as best she could—short dark hair, lined brow, jowly cheeks—and a good likeness emerged on Alissa's pad.

Trouble was, another suspect fit all too well in Maya's brain. Henkes was powerful. Arrogant. Needed to be the center of attention, whether in politics or his own home. And though profiling was designed to identify the type of person who'd done the crimes—not the specific person who'd done them—she couldn't ignore the fact that her profile matched the personality of a man she already knew to be capable of violence against his own son. More importantly, he was tied to at least two of the crime scenes. How could she not consider him a stronger suspect than the man in the picture?

Because coincidence isn't evidence, her conscience warned, *and because you have another reason for wanting it to be Henkes.*

Though she tried like hell to ignore it, the logic spooled through her mind. If Henkes proved to be the Mastermind, she'd eventually be considered a hero for shooting him. At the very least, she'd be back on the force. But the flip side was also true.

If Henkes wasn't the Mastermind, she was finished as a cop.

AFTER SHE REPORTED HER STRANGE phone call to the chief and gave him permission to tap her phone lines, Maya yielded to pressure and spent the night in the guest room of the house Tucker and Alissa had bought together just after their engagement.

She would rather have slept at home, but the Mastermind had shown himself too capable of breaching even the most airtight security.

She woke after dawn, sat up in bed and groaned at the pull of sore muscles and bruised spots. Once she was dressed and more or less ready to face the day, she stumbled downstairs only to find that the house was empty. Warm coffee awaited her, along with a note in Alissa's flowing script. *We've gone to the station. Stay here. I'll be in touch when I can.*

Maya cursed at the sense that she'd gone from house arrest in her own home to house arrest in her friend's home, but her grumble trailed off when she glanced around the rest of the first floor, which she'd been too tired to scope out the night before.

Apparently, the wedding preparations were in full swing. Half-assembled decorations were piled on the table, glittering with Alissa's chosen green-and-silver color scheme. Boxes stacked beneath the table held glass globes that would be filled with green beads and flowers, to act as centerpieces, and a wipe board leaning up against the wall held a seating chart drawn with the precision of a crime scene sketch.

The wedding was—Maya thought quickly—two months away. Where had the time gone? And why hadn't she helped more? Sure, she'd been fitted for her pretty bridesmaid's dress, and she'd made some of the initial arrangements, but in the past few months, nothing.

The realization made her feel even more

shut out, more isolated. Her friendships with Alissa and Cassie were based on shared experiences, shared jobs.

What would happen if they didn't have such things in common anymore?

The sound of a vehicle pulling into the driveway beside the kitchen yanked Maya from her thoughts and sent a spurt of adrenaline through her system. When she recognized Thorne's Interceptor, the adrenaline edged toward something hotter, something more complicated.

She watched him emerge from the car and stride to the kitchen door, and the sight of his semi-familiar face—all hard angles and uncompromising lines in place of the blurred detachment she remembered from before—gathered a hard, hot ball of wanting in her midsection.

"Bad idea." She pressed a hand to her jittering stomach. "Really bad idea."

But that didn't stop her from opening the door before he knocked, and it didn't stop the buzz of pleasure when he tipped down his dark shades and nodded to her shirt. "Nice."

She was still wearing yesterday's jeans, but the blue shirt had been a write-off. She'd scrounged through Alissa's drawers for something that was clingy enough not to hang on her smaller frame, and had wound up with a pale yellow tank top that was far too revealing, so she'd thrown a washed silk blouse over the tank, and tied the tails at her waist. She'd told herself the effect was business casual, but the flare of heat in Thorne's eyes told her she'd misjudged.

Or else she'd lied to herself and dressed to impress a man with just the sort of past she was trying to outrun. A man who could very well turn out to be the chief's choice for her successor.

A man who threatened her on too many levels.

His eyes flicked from her shirt to the house beyond her. "Someone getting married?"

"Alissa and Tucker," she said, grateful for the neutral topic. "Two months from now." She made a face. "I'm a bridesmaid."

He refocused his attention on her. "You don't approve of the marriage?"

She waved him off. "It's not that at all. They're perfect together, even when they're fighting. No, I just don't love weddings in general. Too much fuss over something so personal. That's why I went the Justice of the Peace route."

That and the fact that she'd been a rebellious eighteen, marrying a mid-thirties journalist her parents barely tolerated. Not much to celebrate there.

Thorne returned his shades to the bridge of his nose. "I remember you telling me that." He gestured back to the car. "You ready to go?"

Maya's brain froze as she realized what she'd said. What he'd said. She had casually tossed off a detail from the life she'd left behind, the life she tried damn hard not to think of, and he'd accepted it with a nod. "When did I tell you that?" she asked, before she figured out exactly when that little tidbit must have slipped out.

That night. After the whiskey she barely remembered drinking.

He looked at her sharply. "You don't remember?"

"Of course I remember," she said too quickly. "Never mind, that was..." She shrugged. "Just never mind, okay?" Before he could comment or press, she said, "Where are we going? Back to the station?"

He gave her a long, slow look through his

glasses before he tipped his chin once, as though acknowledging her lie. "Not the station. The prison. We're going to have a chat with Nevada Barnes."

That gave her pause. They were interviewing the Museum Murderer?

"Why bother?" she said, voice sharp with remembered frustration from her own attempts to question Barnes, who had confessed not long after Cassie and Varitek captured him in the museum. "He hasn't exactly been forthcoming in previous interviews. He claims he acted alone, all evidence to the contrary."

"We're bothering because this time he's asked for a meeting. He says he has something to tell us." But Thorne's closed expression told Maya there was more to the story.

She said, "Us as in the Bear Claw PD?"

"No." Thorne shook his head, lips pressed together in a grim line. "As in you and me. He asked for us specifically. And I'll give you one guess how he knew I was involved with the case."

A chill raced through Maya, nerves battling with the hint of a break, with the thought that she was going to be involved in it. "The Mastermind contacted him."

And he'd asked for her by name.

Chapter Six

When they reached the Interceptor, Thorne opened the passenger door for Maya.

She paused and looked up at him with a frown. "I'd prefer it if you didn't hold doors for me. We're not on a date."

"Sorry." He held up his hands and stepped away from the door. "My mother taught me to appreciate seventeenth-century Scottish poetry and hold doors for ladies. It's a habit."

But as he walked around the vehicle while she shut her own door, Thorne admitted privately that he didn't hold doors for every female cop.

Face it—it was just her. She touched something inside him that had gone so long unrecognized that he barely remembered it anymore. She made him think of his mother's dark, lively eyes, his father's military precision and the simpler times when he'd known who he was and what he wanted. That was what had drawn him to her five years earlier.

It drew him still, but he had no right to want her. Not when he hadn't decided whether he was going to do as the chief asked. *Assess her,* the chief had said, *figure out whether she's stable enough to be reinstated to duty, whether in Bear Claw or somewhere else. And for God's sake, keep her away from Wexton Henkes.* It sounded reasonable, but the chief's subtext had been clear.

Give me a good reason to let her go and the job is yours.

There were too many agendas in Bear Claw, too many things designed to distract the police department. Politics, infighting, personnel problems. Hell, Thorne had even picked up a rumor that a few members of the city council were pushing to have Chief Parry himself replaced, though that was patently ludicrous.

In all, the Mastermind couldn't have picked a better year to strike.

"We've got to get focused," Maya said, startling him with the realization that her thoughts had paralleled his.

He pulled out of her street and headed toward the highway, toward the grim penitentiary that straddled the border between Bear Claw and Red Rock. They had a half-hour drive ahead of them, it stood to reason that they should use the time to discuss the case.

Instead, he found himself saying, "Do you want to talk about that night?" When she flinched and turned to him, he shrugged with a forced casualness he suddenly didn't feel. "You browned out, didn't you? How much do you really remember?"

"Enough," she snapped, color riding high in her cheeks. "And no, I don't want to talk about it."

"Suit yourself." He concentrated on driving for a minute, surprised to feel the burn of frustration. With her. With himself. He needed to focus, and not just on the case. But that was a good place to start, so as he turned onto the main highway, he said, "Okay, here's your chance. I'm a captive audience. Tell me why you think Henkes is the Mastermind."

It was her turn to fall silent. She crossed her arms and stared out the window at the scenery as it transitioned from the well-planned city of Bear Claw to the deep, dark greenery of the Bear Claw Canyon State Park. They rolled past the section of the park where Bradford Croft had kept the kidnapped girls, the place where he'd nearly killed Alissa before Tucker had come to her rescue.

They had passed the park entrance before Maya finally drew breath and said, "Henkes's son was admitted to Hawthorne Hospital twice in two weeks for unrelated, suspicious injuries. I tried to build a case, but the evidence didn't hold. All I had were a few inconsistent statements from the wife and son, and the kid's medical records. Neither of the family members would press charges, the judge is one of Henkes's tennis buddies, and after what I did…" She lifted one shoulder. "No case."

"So you decided to go after him for something else."

"No," she snapped, "I'm not blinded by him the way the others in this community have been. I'm not ready to kiss his butt because he's some local boy done good who's throwing money around now." She paused and lowered her voice. "Look, let's consider them two separate cases for a minute. Granted, I wouldn't have looked at Henkes in the first place if it hadn't been for Child Services calling me in when Kier—" she stumbled on the name, "when his son wound up hospitalized for a fractured wrist. But let's say for a moment that Henkes developed as a suspect through other channels."

Though he thought she was seriously reaching, Thorne nodded. "So stipulated."

She twisted her hands together in her lap. "Once I started looking at Henkes, I found that he's involved with the state park commission and the board of the Natural History Museum. While just about anyone could get into the state park, the museum was closed for renovations when Nevada Barnes lured Cassie and Varitek inside and tried to kill them. Barnes had keys and the proper codes, but we've never figured out where he got them. Then there was the attack on the Chuckwagon Ranch yesterday. Henkes is a part owner of the place."

"Sounds thin," Thorne said bluntly. "There's nothing to say that a board member would've had access, either. And it doesn't make sense to say that Henkes would be targeting his own properties. If anything, the reverse would be true. Maybe the attacks on Henkes's properties indicate that he's become a target."

"That's—" Maya stopped herself, and then grudgingly said, "That's possible, I suppose. Damn it." She scowled. "I know it sounds strange, but I want..." She trailed off.

"You want it to be Henkes because if he's the Mastermind, you're vindicated," Thorne said. "What is now being played like a cop attacking an influential private citizen in his own home becomes a psych specialist one step ahead of her own superiors. You'd be a hero."

She turned back to the window and her voice was small when she said, "I don't want to be a hero. I just want to be back on the job."

He wanted to tell her there was no chance, that the chief had already made up his mind to shuffle her off the Bear Claw force, the only question remaining was whether she could carry a badge while she did paperwork somewhere else. But even as that impulse formed, Thorne turned into the Red Rock Penitentiary and drove through the narrow, guarded tunnel that formed the first layer of containment for the prisoners. The tunnel lights were sodium-based, casting the road in orangey brown light.

Orangey brown. Brown-out. The thoughts connected in his brain with an uncomfortable click.

He remembered how quickly she'd gotten hammered on four fingers of whiskey at his place. Later, when she passed out half across his bed with tear tracks drying on her cheeks, he'd figured she'd started early. Hey, it was Friday. He wasn't going to judge her for being a lightweight.

But now he might have to do just that.

What if she'd been drinking the day she went after Wexton Henkes? The reports said she'd arrived unannounced and seemed normal enough when she'd asked to speak with Henkes. But once they were seated in the living room, Henkes claimed she'd become argumentative, then outright violent. She'd pulled her weapon, and when Henkes had tried to disarm her, the firearm had discharged and he'd been shot in the arm. Maya had fallen and struck her head, leaving her in a semi-comatose state for nearly three days.

At least that was what the reports said, and the evidence was more or less consistent with the story. But with Henkes the only eyewitness…

Could the truth lie somewhere else?

Deep in thought, Thorne parked the Interceptor in the inner lot of the prison, the parking area closest to the outer wall that separated the courtyards from the cell blocks, overlooked by manned towers at each corner.

He climbed out of the car, needing to move, to pace. Apparently sensing something was up, Maya joined him, then leaned back against the car and folded her arms across her chest. "What is it?"

Thorne took a deep breath and tried to decide whether he was asking because it might help the case, or because it would help him take her job. The latter thought brought a sting of guilt, one that had grown stronger every hour since he'd first realized whose job he'd been offered. It didn't matter that the chief was going to replace her one way or another, Thorne owed her better than to scheme behind her back.

Unable to deal with the dilemma right then, he said, "Look, I can't think of a graceful way to ask this, but is it possible that you were drunk when you went to Wexton Henkes's house?" When she hissed in a breath and her eyes darkened to storms, he held up a hand. "I'm not judging or anything. Lord knows I have no right. But it was obvious earlier that you don't remember much," maybe anything, "about that night back at the academy. You were pretty plastered." He jammed his hands in his pockets and tipped his head down, so he could look at her over the tops of his shades. "You can tell me, you know. I can help you deal with it. I can—"

"I don't need your help," she said, voice low. Embarrassed color rode high on her cheekbones and a pulse pounded along the slim column of her neck. "I didn't... I don't—" She broke off with a quiet curse, pushed away from the car and headed for the prison security checkpoint, a clear signal that the conversation was over.

But before Thorne could follow, she spun

back, eyes blazing. "No, damn it. I'm going to say this." She took a breath and said, "You're right, I don't remember that night in High Top Bluff. Nothing after that first drink. So I don't know if I told you that I developed an allergy to alcohol when I was nineteen, that I brown out practically at the first taste." Her lips twisted in a bloodless, humorless smile. "I wasn't always that way. I could keep up with the best of them until—" She broke off, a shadow crossing her face. "Never mind. Not important. What's important is that yes, I browned out on you. But I'll also have you know that until that night with you, I hadn't touched a drop in six years." Her hand lifted to touch her throat. "And I've been dry in the five years since. That night was..." She lifted her shoulders helplessly. "I don't know what that night was."

"It was a mistake," he said, feeling the slap of grief, of guilt. He'd been buzzed enough that the voices in his head had been dulled to a background roar, buzzed enough that he'd wanted her to join him in a drink. At the time, he'd thought her protests forced, but once the tears started, he realized he'd been the one doing the forcing. Or at least the persuading. Just a little drink, he'd said. Don't you want to keep me company?

If he'd known…

Hell, it wouldn't have changed anything. That was the sort of man he'd been back then. The sort of man she'd saved him from being. But in the process, he'd taken more from her than he'd intended.

"My mistake," she said, agreeing with him and challenging him at the same time. "My responsibility. I chose to drink your whiskey. I chose to do—" She faltered and looked away. "Whatever we did."

"Nothing," Thorne said quietly. When she looked at him, eyes bleak, he said, "We didn't do anything. We talked. You passed out. I tucked you in. End of story."

He left out the part where he'd sat up late into the night, watching her sleep and trying to figure out what to say to her when she woke up, how to convince her they could heal together. He also left out the part about how he'd woken up alone and cursed her for it, how he'd gone looking for her and felt like he'd been kicked in the chest when he realized she'd run.

She sucked in a breath. "We didn't…"

"No, we didn't." He saw the relief in her eyes and felt a spurt of frustrated anger. But he couldn't blame her for thinking what she'd thought. He hadn't been much of a gentleman back then. Still wasn't, for that matter, despite his mother's best efforts, which is why he pressed now, asking her, "You said you've been dry since. How about the night you went to Henkes's place and shot him in the arm? Did you drink that night? Is that why you can't remember the struggle, and why were out of it for three days after?"

"No," she said, quietly. "I didn't drink that night. I swear it."

But he thought he caught a flicker in the back of her eyes, confusion maybe, or doubt. He took a step forward, needing to know. "Maya, talk to me. I can help."

Almost without conscious volition, he lifted a hand to move a strand of dark hair away from her cheek. His finger grazed her soft flesh.

And an image ripped through his carefully constructed barriers and nearly brought him to his knees.

MAYA SAW HIM FLINCH. HIS skin grayed and his eyes went dark with shock and something else. Maybe fear.

Her angry shame gave ground to concern. "Thorne? Are you okay?" She reached for him, thinking to guide him to the car, to the curb, before he fell.

"Don't touch me!" He staggered back, reeled and nearly fell before he was able to brace his legs and stand, breathing quickly, hands clutching at his sides.

Then he took a long, shuddering breath and his eyes cleared. His hands stilled.

And his expression darkened with a dread emotion she couldn't define.

"Thorne?" she said, taking a small step backward, away from him. She'd never seen him look so grim. So violent.

Then the darkness was gone, blanked from his eyes and face so thoroughly she might have imagined it. He blinked twice, straightened to his normal stance, cleared his throat and nodded to the checkpoint guarding the entrance to the next layer of prison security. "You ready to talk to Barnes?"

Maya stood her ground. "I'm not letting you off that easy. What the hell just happened?"

He jammed his hands in his pockets and started walking. "Nothing."

Instead of grabbing him, she ducked around in front of him and blocked his path. When he stopped and glared, she crossed her arms and lifted her chin. "Try again." Remembering the rumors of why he'd been assigned to a teaching rotation, how he'd gone undercover and come out with post-traumatic stress disorder and delusions of ESP, she said, "Did you have a flashback?"

His lips twisted in a smile that was utterly devoid of humor. "I haven't had a flash in five years."

His words echoed her own—*I haven't had a drink in five years*—and the look in his eye told her it was intentional.

He was lying to her just as she had lied to him.

That made them even.

Or did it?

Minutes later, Maya found herself on the wrong side of a sheet of one-way glass. The corrections officer who'd escorted her to the narrow, gunmetal-gray viewing room gestured to the dark glass panel that took up most of one wall. "They'll bring up the lights in just a minute and you'll be able to see the interview room. The volume control for the speakers is down there on the right."

"Thanks," Maya said, trying to keep her voice friendly because it wasn't his fault Thorne had suddenly changed his mind and decided he didn't want her in on the interview. She wasn't sure whether he was punishing her for their argument out in the parking lot, or if he'd developed another theory, but he'd been immovable on the decision.

The corrections officer nodded and closed the door behind him when he left. A lock clicked into place, and moments later the lights came up in the adjoining room, which was painted the same gunmetal gray as her room, and held a bolted-down table and two chairs.

Thorne stood behind the table, staring at her. She knew he couldn't see her, knew he was probably staring into space, thinking of the coming interview. But his intense gaze locked on hers through the one-way glass as though he knew precisely where she was, precisely what she was thinking.

She felt the click of connection, felt a

spear of heat in her core, and cursed herself for the weakness that drew her to bad-ass men, the sort who drank and lied and manipulated the truth to suit their needs.

The good guys she'd dated had left her cold, while the damaged, angry ones made her burn.

And left her charred in the aftermath.

"My choice, my responsibility," she said aloud, and as though he'd heard her through the one-way audio hookup, Thorne looked away, breaking the connection.

They both heard the clang and bang of the far door being opened, the one connected to the prison itself. Thorne leaned up against the wall with his arms folded over his chest and a bored expression on his face.

Nevada Barnes appeared in the doorway, flanked by two guards.

Seeming small in his orange prison jumpsuit, the gaunt-faced Barnes shuffled toward the table, his slow, short strides making him look as though he was shackled, though his wrists and ankles were bare of chains. His narrow shoulders were hunched, his body thinner than the last time Maya had seen him, when she'd sat at the back of the room during his arraignment and tried to figure out what made him tick. What made him kill.

Which parts of the plan had been his and which had come from his master.

Barnes sank into the flimsy plastic chair at his side of the bolted-down table. His orange jumpsuit settled around him, like a deflating balloon, making him look empty. Hollow. Dried-out, as though something else had been animating him from within while he'd committed the crimes.

"I got a message that you were ready to talk to me," Thorne said. He didn't move from his position against the wall, keeping the high ground as the guards backed out of the room and closed the door.

Barnes turned his head and looked toward the reflective glass. "I said I was ready to talk to the shrink." He spoke slowly, as though each word was an effort. "Not you, though. The woman. The pretty one. Maya."

The air chilled in her viewing room, and goose bumps shivered to life on her arms. The murderer's eyes fixed far to the left of her, and when his lips curved strangely, his attention was focused on…nothing.

"She couldn't make it," Thorne said.

"You'll have to deal with me or nobody." He dropped into the chair opposite Barnes, and his voice warmed a notch. "Look, Nevada, I've read your file. I can tell you're not a bad guy. You're a decent man who had a rough childhood and fell in with the wrong sort of influences. You were just doing what you were told, right? So why not let me help you?"

Maya saw a muscle tic at the corner of Thorne's jaw. Barnes was every inch the "bad guy." When childhood abuse had put him over the edge, he'd killed his father in a staged hunting accident, and taken off with his stepmother, who had then posed as the young man's wife for several years before she, too, met an untimely end. The Bear Claw PD was still trying to fill in where Barnes had spent the next decade before he'd resurfaced in Bear Claw and started hunting the prey dictated by the Mastermind.

Barnes's eyes slid away from the reflective glass and returned to Thorne. "No, cop. I'm trying to help *you,* but I can't. Not until you let me talk to her."

Thorne stared at him for a long minute, then pressed his palms flat to the table and leaned toward the killer. "Look, here's the deal. She's been suspended. She's not on active duty anymore, and there's no way I can bring her in on this. I'm sorry, but you're going to have to deal with me."

"Then I have nothing to say." The words were suddenly deep and powerful, as though they'd come from someone other than the hollowed-out killer sitting at the table in a too-large orange jumpsuit.

Thorne stood. "Let me know when you're really ready to deal." He slapped a button on the wall beside the exit door, and the guards hustled through the prison-side door to sweep Barnes from the room.

Halfway out, the confessed murderer turned back and called, "Think about it, Coleridge. You get me access to the woman and I guarantee you won't be disappointed."

Then he was gone, taking his information with him.

Anger rising, Maya slammed through the viewing room door and confronted Thorne in the hallway. She didn't touch him, but she got right in his face. "You should have called me in. If he has information for us—"

"Not here," he snapped, and headed for the security check.

Fuming, she hurried to catch up. Once they were outside, crossing the strip of concrete that separated the main building from the outer wall, she said, "What the hell has gotten in to you? If this is about what happened earlier, then get over it. You're acting unprofessionally."

Thorne spun in his tracks near a parked prison van. "Don't you dare lecture me about unprofessional behavior." He leaned closer, until she saw the pulse throbbing at the base of his throat and felt the spiky energy dance in the air that separated them. Nearly whispering, he said, "And ask yourself this: how did he know to ask for both of us by name? Why wasn't he surprised to hear that you'd been suspended?"

Maya stilled as the data snippets lined up in her brain. "He's getting information from someone on the outside. Someone connected."

Thorne nodded. "Exactly."

She spun back toward the prison, where the guards were marching Barnes across the courtyard, back to his cell. "Then I should talk to him. Now."

"Wait." He reached out, but didn't touch

her. When she stopped beside the prison van, he let his hand fall. His eyes were dark and enigmatic when he said, "You will talk to him, I promise. We'll be going back in there in a few minutes. That'll let him feel like he won, and it'll give us time to go over a few things."

"Why out here?" she asked, gesturing at the open air and the guard towers that loomed above them. "Not much in the way of ambiance."

"Not much in the way of opportunities for someone to overhear our conversation," he countered. He jerked his chin toward the curtain wall of the prison. "Think about it. If the Mastermind has someone transmitting up-to-the-minute PD information to Barnes, it could be—"

A shot split the air, severing his words. The driver's window in the prison van beside Maya cracked with the impact of a bullet.

She heard another shot. A shout of pain.

And everything went to hell.

Chapter Seven

Thorne grabbed Maya as the van window shattered. Small fragments of glass peppered them both, stinging his neck and the top of his right shoulder. He took two running steps toward the security checkpoint, then stopped.

It was too far. They'd never make it across the wide expanse of concrete. They'd be sitting ducks. He reversed direction and shoved her behind the van as shots three and four slammed into the vehicle.

He risked a peek around the front grille and saw a glint of sunlight, a shadow of furtive movement. He heard shouts and chaos from within the prison, and the pop of a handgun as the guards returned fire.

"The shots are coming from the northeast guard tower," Thorne said tersely. A fifth bullet sizzled over the top of the van, angling down to shatter on the cement wall at their backs.

He winced as shrapnel dug a fiery path into his shoulder. Maya grabbed on to the forearm he'd crossed protectively over her chest, and tried to shove him away. "Why aren't you returning fire?"

"The guards have it covered. We'll just sit tight." It went against his training and his nature, but he'd long ago learned that each prison had its own hierarchy.

He heard another shot from inside the curtain wall. Curses and a man's cry of pain. Damned if it didn't sound like the sniper's attack had moved into the penitentiary itself.

What the hell was going on? Maya was the target.

Wasn't she?

The gunshot echoes died quickly, though the shouts and whistles increased. Someone within the prison finally hit the general alarm, adding the whoop of a siren to the din.

Thorne heard running footsteps. He cursed and spun, grabbing for his weapon, then relaxed his fighting stance when he saw one of the corrections officers jogging toward them. Thorne raised his voice and called, "What's the situation inside?"

The corrections officer was in his mid-forties, fit and tough-looking like so many of his breed. The tag clipped to his breast pocket identified him as Graves, Samuel. He jerked his head toward the security checkpoint. "I think you'll want to see this."

Maya pushed ahead of Thorne. "Do you have an on-site medical staff?"

"Of course. They're with the injured man right now." Graves had to stretch his legs to keep up with her, leaving Thorne in their wake.

Thorne's back ached like fury and his legs wouldn't carry him as fast as he wanted to go. His feet felt like crumbling cement blocks he was being forced to drag through thigh-deep water.

Reaction, he told himself. It was an adrenaline backlash, nothing more. But by the time they'd passed through the security checkpoint and reentered the prison, Thorne knew it was more than that. The smell of blood filled his nostrils and suffused his brain. The iron tang reminded him of rage and pain, and a man being strangled to death high in the mountains.

Worse, he saw the ghostly part-images of events he hadn't lived yet. Blood. Death.

A woman's scream.

"Thorne?" Maya's voice seemed to come from far away. "Thorne, what's wrong?"

He saw her face at the end of a long tunnel, took a step toward her, but she seemed to draw further away. He heard her say, "Oh hell, he's bleeding. Grab him, he's hurt."

He wanted to tell her it wasn't the cuts on his back sapping his strength, it was the wounds on his brain, the lesions created by the drugs Mason Falk had pumped into him.

Were the visions flashbacks or prescience? He'd never known, and he'd been glad when he'd finally conquered them, when his brain had finally healed enough to free him from the madness.

Or so he'd thought.

The darkness closed in, gripping his consciousness and squeezing tight until his legs folded. Helping hands guided him to the ground. His senses cut out one by one, smell and taste first, then sight. But he could still feel Maya's gentle touch.

And he could still hear the corrections officer say, "Nevada Barnes took a bullet to the brain. He's dead."

MAYA WASN'T SURE WHICH was more shocking—that the Museum Murderer had been gunned down not a hundred yards from her, or that Thorne had collapsed. Barnes's execution was a shock that she hadn't yet fully grasped. But Thorne's condition was inexplicable.

He remained in a semi-conscious, almost trancelike state as he sat cross-legged on the pavement of the prison courtyard, some twenty yards from where a widening pool of blood seeped from beneath Barnes's body on the other side of a sturdy wire fence. In the near distance, the shouts of the inmates diminished as the corrections officers quelled the brief chaos within the penitentiary. Further away, she heard the rising sound of sirens, heralding the arrival of reinforcements for a scene that was already secure.

Or was it? Maya straightened suddenly and looked toward the corner guard tower where the shots had originated. She glanced at Samuel Graves, the corrections officer who'd come running to tell them Barnes had been killed. "Please tell me you got the shooter."

Graves's lips drew tight in a thin line that answered her question even before he said, "We got the gun, but by the time we reached the tower, the bastard was gone."

"Impossible," Maya protested, though it was clearly more than possible. It had happened. "This is a prison. How could the shooter simply walk out?"

"Maybe he didn't," Thorne's voice said from close beside her ear.

She gasped and spun, shocked to find him standing beside her, clear-eyed, and stunned by the sizzle that zapped through her at the touch of his breath at her jaw, the low rasp of his voice in her ear.

Struggling to cover her response, she said, "Sit down before you fall, Thorne."

"I'm fine," he responded flatly, not even looking at her. His eyes were fixed on the guard tower.

"You should have those cuts looked at, seeing as you lost enough blood to drop you, even for a few minutes." But when she walked around him to get a better look at the bloody streaks showing through his torn shirt, it didn't seem as though he'd lost much volume at all.

"It wasn't the—" He broke off and cursed. "The scratches are nothing. I'll deal with them later. Right now we need to figure out who shot at us and killed Nevada Barnes."

And why, Maya almost said, but she didn't bother because the answer was obvious. She and Thorne hadn't been the main focus of the attack. Barnes had been the target. He'd been gunned down as he'd crossed the courtyard that separated the interrogation area from the general population cells. Two shots to the brain and *poof,* he was gone.

"The Mastermind didn't want him talking to us," Maya said softly. "Didn't want him talking to *me.* Or did he?" She frowned, thinking. "Why tell Barnes to ask for both of us, then prevent him from talking? It doesn't make any sense." She slid a glance up at Thorne and saw a muscle pulse beside his jaw. "If you'd called me into the room in the first place, we might have gotten something."

The muscle twitched harder and Thorne scowled. "What's done is done." He turned toward the body. "Come on. Let's get whatever information we can from the Red Rock cops, then head back to Bear Claw. Chief Parry needs to hear about this." Then he glanced back toward the guard tower, and a shadow passed across his face. "We'll need access to a fax machine. I'd like to show Alissa's sketch to a few people."

A chill skittered through Maya's gut. "You think the guy who snatched little Hannah and tried to hit you with the delivery van might have been an inmate here?"

"Maybe, maybe not. But it's worth checking out."

An hour later, they had their answer. The van driver wasn't an ex-con. He was a prison guard named Drew Wilson.

And he was AWOL.

IT WAS WELL PAST DARK BEFORE Maya and Thorne headed back to Bear Claw. They had dug into Drew Wilson's employment records—which were scant, since he'd been hired on at the Red Rock Pen only *after* Nevada Barnes's incarceration, and they'd ridden along as the Red Rock cops—who had jurisdiction—checked his listed address and found a sub shop instead.

Some progress. A few dead ends. A very long day.

Maya had watched Thorne grow increasingly uncomfortable as the hours passed. He had pulled a light windbreaker out of his car and used it to cover the bloody stripes on his back, but they were clearly paining him.

Hell, for all she knew, he was still carrying shards of cement or glass in there. He'd waved off her suggestion that he let the ambulance attendants tend his wounds. He'd grunted in the negative when the prison doctor had offered to take a look, and snarled when Maya had pressed.

By the time they finally reached his vehicle out in the parking lot, she'd had it with his machismo. "I'm driving."

She took it as a measure of his discomfort that he didn't argue. Instead, he muttered a soft curse and levered himself into the passenger seat.

Without discussing it, she drove to her building and parked in the underground garage. The Bear Claw cops had bugged the phones in her condo and Tucker had called in a favor and gotten a state-of-the-art security system installed that morning. The place was as safe as it could be.

"Come upstairs," she said, and winced when the words came out in a husky voice that didn't sound like hers at all. She forced a stronger, more practical tone and said, "We'll get you cleaned up before we report in."

She climbed out of the car without waiting for an answer, opened his door and reached down to help him lever himself out of the passenger's seat.

"I've got it," he grumbled, and once he was on his feet, he slammed the door for emphasis.

But he didn't argue the detour.

As they walked across the dark garage to the locked elevator lobby, he stayed close to her. She was aware of the tension in his frame, the protective glares he sent into the shadows, and she realized all over again that the danger hadn't passed with the death of Nevada Barnes.

They had an APB out on Drew Wilson, but he could be anywhere. On the run.

On the hunt.

Maya glanced into the shadows and

moved closer to Thorne as she keyed them into the elevator lobby. Even hurt, he was a formidable opponent.

But once they were upstairs, inside her suddenly small-feeling condo, she was forced to admit that he was formidable, period. He dominated the space, making the small touches of decor more feminine than she'd intended. He prowled from room to room as he had the day before, looking for an intruder. When he was done, he faced her and raised an eyebrow. "You want me in the bathroom?"

His expression was challenging, as if to say, *This was your idea.*

Yes it was, she acknowledged, beginning to think she would've been better off taking him to the ER. She'd thought she was strong enough to handle having him in her space.

Maybe she'd been wrong.

"I can barely fit in the bathroom alone, never mind with someone else." Face hot, she turned away and gestured to the kitchen nook. "In there. Pull up a stool at the breakfast bar. The light's good enough for your *superficial* cuts." She emphasized the word, hoping for reassurance, or maybe an explanation.

She still didn't understand his collapse. If it hadn't been from the cuts, then what?

"Will do." He shrugged out of his wind-breaker, baring the torn back of his shirt, which was streaked with rusty brown now that the stains had set.

When he lifted his hands to the buttons, Maya escaped to the bathroom and let out a long, whistling breath.

Bringing him home had seemed like a good idea when he'd refused treatment at the prison and turned down a ride to the ER. But as she flattened her palms against the cool lip of the sink and stared at herself in the mirror, she had to wonder if she honestly knew what she was doing.

She pressed her lips together, and in the reflection, her mouth thinned to a determined line. "I'm just patching him up so we can head to the station and figure out what comes next. That's all."

But it felt like more than that when she stripped her bathroom of first aid supplies, and noticed that her fingers trembled very slightly. It felt like more than that when she had to stop and take a deep breath before opening the door, in an effort to slow her rocketing heartbeat and quell the jumpy nerves in her stomach.

And it felt like more when she stepped out into the main living space and saw Thorne sitting on one of her breakfast bar stools, bare-chested.

His shoulders were broad and well defined, carrying the strength of a man who was naturally powerful, maybe from gym work, maybe from life. A light fuzz of coarse hair drew her attention to the slope of his tautly muscled chest and the contours of his ribs and abdominal muscles below, forming a washboard sculpture that urged her fingers to touch, to trace.

He'd turned on the overhead kitchen fluorescents, which usually felt too bright to her, but now seemed exactly perfect as they splashed light across his torso, washing his natural tan to a pearly white that made her think of statues and fine art.

As she watched, he reached behind him and scooped up a glass half full of clear liquid. Tipped it to his lips. Drained it.

And her heart stopped.

She saw the bottle on the breakfast bar. Saw the knowing twitch of his lips when he noticed her standing just inside the main room. "If you haven't taken a drink in five years, why's there an open bottle of rum front and center in your pasta cabinet?"

She stalked to the breakfast bar and slammed the medical supplies down onto the mosaic tile surface. "It's a reminder. A symbol. Proof that I can be tempted without giving in."

He set the glass down with a clink. "Then why is it open?"

The smell of rum permeated the air, working its way into her nostrils like an old friend.

She shuddered at a surge of want that carried the strength of arousal and the disgust of nausea. "None of your damn business. You want me to clean those cuts or not?"

He stared at her for a long moment before he turned away, presenting his back, which was streaked with ugly, scabbed-over wounds. "Go ahead, but do me a favor and don't use the rum as a disinfectant. I'm going to need it for anesthesia."

"Nice to see one of us still likes his booze," she said tartly. Then she pressed her lips together and blew out a breath. "Sorry. None of my business."

He was silent while she stepped into the kitchen and drew a pan of warm water, then dumped enough disinfectant in to turn the water blood-red. She returned to where he sat, soaked a half-dozen gauze pads in the mixture, and used the first to wipe at the bloody streaks on his back.

She winced. "This looks like hell."

"Some of it's old." His voice was carefully neutral, but the muscles of his neck and shoulders tightened.

She looked closer and saw that the bloody scabs on his right shoulder and the palm-sized bruise along his ribs were new. But the puckered scar tissue lower down was old, as were the dark stripes that crossed his spine and ran diagonally down to the belted waistband of his slacks. Maya brushed the tough, dark skin with her fingertips. When he flinched, she pulled back. "Sorry."

"Doesn't matter," he said shortly. "It was a long time ago." But the cords of his neck stood out in sharp relief and he swallowed hard, the sound and motion seeming amplified in the quiet kitchen with its bright, unforgiving light.

As Maya cleaned the shallow cuts and

used a pair of tweezers to work small shards of glass and cement out of his back, she was conscious of the warm, tight skin beneath her hands, conscious of Thorne's steady breathing and the scent of man overlaid by those of rum and blood.

After a long moment, he surprised her by saying, "I started drinking after I came down off the mountain. I'm sure you know the story. It was more or less common knowledge at the academy."

"I know some of it," Maya said. She wasn't sure why he'd brought it up. Maybe guilt for laying her raw. Maybe something else. "You went undercover to infiltrate Mason Falk's cult up in the Wagon Ridge Mountains and something went wrong."

He snorted, but there was no mirth in the sound. "Close enough. They broke my cover—maybe I slipped up, maybe someone on the force turned, we never figured it out. They grabbed me out of my bed and chained me in what Falk called the 'correction chamber.' It was where he put the women and children who went against the tenets of his so-called faith." He shrugged, then winced when the motion pulled at the clean, weepy cuts on his back. "He didn't put the men in there. Them, he killed. Except in my case, he needed me alive. He needed information. How much the PD knew. When they were planning to raid—he knew it was a case of when, not if."

He fell silent. Maya ripped open a package of butterfly bandages and winced at the noise, which seemed too loud, too violent in the overbright kitchen.

Thorne flinched, then, as she began to apply the bandages, he continued, "I was held captive for two and a half days. Sixty of the longest hours of my life. Part of Falk's 'religion' involved snake venom and hallucinogens, and he pumped me full of whatever he had on hand, trying to get me to talk." His voice grew raw. "Hell, there were times I would've talked, just to make him stop, but I couldn't remember the answers anymore. I didn't even know my own name. He'd stripped me bare, layer by layer, going deep, deeper than maybe he meant. In the end, there wasn't much left of me except—" His hands flexed on his wool-clad knees and he swallowed. "Let's just say it wasn't pretty."

Maya was done with his back, but she kept dabbing with a gauze pad, unwilling to face him square-on, unwilling to let him see the look of horror on her face.

Maybe unwilling to see his.

When she'd known him in the academy, he'd been maybe six months removed from his ordeal. His eyes had been hunted, haunted and blurred at the edges by the whiskey he drank when he thought nobody was looking.

"I spent a few days in the hospital, then released myself. I wasn't badly injured— some burns and cuts, a couple of broken fingers. But the drugs and the venom had done a number on me. I had...spells. Visions. I don't know what to call them, even to this day." His voice grew raw. "Sometimes I'd see things I'd done. Sometimes things I was going to do. Awful things." He reached for the glass on the marble countertop, lifted it and drained the last few drops. "I tried therapy, tried hypnosis, tried tranquilizers, acupuncture, homeopathy...hell, I even looked into electroshock. But for those first six months, whiskey was the only thing that blocked the flashes."

Sympathy gave way to a snap of temper. "Which makes it okay to drink your breakfast?" She stepped away from him and collected the first aid supplies with an angry swipe. "Do you have any idea what that does to your body? To the people around you? Have you ever seen—"

She broke off, knowing her sudden anger wasn't about him.

It was about her. About what Dane had done.

What she'd done.

Thorne turned to face her, and there was something new in his eyes. A softness she didn't understand, didn't deserve. "Yeah, I have. That's why I decided to tough it out on my own, without the chemical props. I tried meditation. Martial arts. Working out. Whatever it took to keep me tired, to keep the flashes at bay." He lifted one shoulder, causing the muscles to ripple beneath his tight skin. "Though I'm not strictly sober, I haven't had a drink in a while."

Maya nodded to the empty glass. "Then why have one tonight?"

His eyes darkened. "Damned if I know." He scrubbed a hand across his face, and when he looked at her again, there was new awareness in his expression. "Yes, I do know. It was..." He trailed off as though seeking the right words. "It was a knee-jerk reaction against something I couldn't control. It won't happen again."

Though there was truth in his eyes, in his voice, Maya had heard the words a thousand times before. "That's what they all say."

Thorne smiled, though with little humor. "I'm not the one with the open bottle in her kitchen cabinet."

"Touché." She gestured to his ripped shirt and windbreaker, which he'd looped over the second bar stool. "Get dressed while I scrounge you some aspirin. Then we can hit the PD and see whether there's been any progress on finding Drew Wilson."

But when she moved to pass him, he reached out with his arm and blocked her path. He stood, looming over her too close, too bare chested. "Wait. I want to thank you. And apologize. I have no right to criticize you."

Maya felt the warmth of his body and tasted the hint of man and rum on the air. She shifted, but held her ground. "You're welcome. And as far as the apology..." She shrugged. "I think we're pretty much even in that regard. The fact that we knew each other before makes things complicated. We weren't really friends. We weren't lovers." Thank you, God. "But we were—" She blew out a breath, frustrated. "Hell, we weren't really anything, were we?"

"We were the possibility of something to come," he said quietly. "At least I thought we were."

Maya blew out a breath. "You can't actually have believed—"

His lips twisted with zero humor. "Clearly, you didn't." He spread his hands, causing the muscles in his bare arms to bunch and shift. "I noticed you in class. You tried to keep a low profile, but I noticed you. If you hadn't broken down that night…" He trailed off, then continued. "I don't know if I would've approached you. I was a mess, not good for anyone, including myself. Then your battery died and you needed a ride home and the rest is history."

For some more than others, Maya thought. She wished she knew what had happened that night. She was glad to know they hadn't had sex, but she worried what else she might have done. What she might have said.

Something had created a strange sense of intimacy between them, even though they were nearly strangers. She wished she knew what it was. She tipped her chin down, trying to find the right words to ask.

He nudged her face back up with a forefinger, and the contact sent a buzz through her system. It was the first time he'd intentionally touched her, the first time he hadn't flinched away.

"Why did you run?"

The look in his eyes stripped away her pretenses, leaving her with the bare truth. Without consciously processing the words, she said, "Because I wasn't strong enough to resist you and I knew it. Booze. Sex. Love. I would have given in to all of it, and that would have been a disaster."

His eyes darkened and he withdrew an inch. "A disaster for whom?"

"For both of us," she snapped. "Why don't you see it? What do you remember about that night that I don't?"

A look of pain, or maybe resignation, crossed his handsome features. "This."

And he kissed her.

Chapter Eight

On one level, Maya wasn't surprised to taste Thorne on her lips and feel his strong arms curl around her. A deep, womanly core within her acknowledged the attraction, the compulsion.

But on another level she was shocked. Not by the fact of the kiss, but by what it did to her.

It made her *feel*.

After her wild adolescence, after Dane and her disaster of a marriage, she'd buffered herself against attraction, against the wild hormones that swept away rationality. She didn't trust that slap of heat and need, the surge of sexual gratification that felt too much like being buzzed. But in that first instant of contact, that first brush of lips and touch of tongue and breath, Thorne swept past those barriers and reached far inside her, asking for a response. Demanding one.

She gasped at the flare of heat, the wash of power. He swallowed the small sound and swept his tongue inside her mouth as she gripped his bare shoulders and hung on for the ride.

He cupped his palms at her hips, urging her toward him, or maybe restraining her from leaving. But there was no thought of retreat—not now, not when she savored the faint flavor of alcohol on his breath and found the taste of the man beneath, rich and flavorful, compelling and powerful.

Both tastes set off warning bells, but the sound was lost amidst the heat.

She returned the kiss, encouraged it, reveled in it. Warmth flowered within her, spiraling out from her core, kindled by nothing more than the touch of his lips. She murmured his name, or maybe he said hers, she wasn't sure and it didn't seem to matter.

Wanting the closeness, the contact, she slid her hands down to where his rested at her waist. He turned his hands to meet hers, to align with hers, palm to palm, and allow their fingers to intertwine. She squeezed his hands, seeking reassurance, seeking something—

He stiffened and jerked away from her, though his fingers remained clamped on hers, tightening painfully. His eyes went wide and unfocused.

"Thorne, what's wrong?" She tugged on their joined hands, and excitement morphed to a prickle of fear when he didn't respond. "Let go, you're hurting me."

She yanked harder. He released her abruptly, and she stumbled back, arms windmilling as she fought to keep her balance. But he didn't lunge forward to help. He just stood there.

Slowly, his eyes refocused. His hands clenched into fists. And he said a single word. *"Maya."*

A chill ran through her at the sound of his voice. She fought to shift gears even as she realized she'd nearly fallen back into that old, destructive pattern. Instant gratification. No self-control. She folded her arms across her chest. Inwardly, she vowed it wouldn't happen again. She had to be tougher than temptation. Stronger than addiction.

But aloud, she said, "You had one of those visions, didn't you? What did you see?"

He grabbed his shirt, pulled it on and buttoned it over his chest. "They're not visions. They're just flashbacks. The hallucinogenic drugs linger in the spinal fluid for years. A chance move, a muscle spasm, hell, just random bad luck releases a small bit of fluid into the bloodstream and *wham!* I'm right back there, in that crummy room with Falk and his right-hand man, Donny Greek."

Maya's chest constricted. "Is that what you saw?"

He shook his head. "I don't know what I saw. It's been so long... I thought the flashes were gone. I thought I'd beaten them." He grabbed his jacket. "I'm going to take off. Do some driving. Do some thinking. I'll report back to Chief Parry and set up a meeting for the three of us in the morning." He was back-pedaling as he spoke. Running.

Anger rose in Maya's chest, born of self-disgust that she'd given in to temptation, mixed with hurt that he could leave her so easily after the kiss.

She nodded toward the breakfast bar. "You want to take the bottle with you for the drive?"

His face blanked, letting her know she'd scored a direct hit. But his voice was carefully neutral when he said. "Keep it. You never know when the urge will strike."

As he walked away, she had a feeling he wasn't talking about the whiskey anymore.

He turned back with one hand on the doorknob. "Stay inside until I come for you tomorrow morning. Don't leave the condo. Use the machine to screen your calls, and contact me if you see or hear anything odd." He cursed. "Call me if you even feel like something's off. Got it?"

She lifted her chin in a gesture that she hoped came across as dismissive, even though it felt stiff and plastic. "I'll call the chief. He can decide whether to keep you in the loop."

They traded a long, silent stare before Thorne nodded sharply. "As you wish." Then he pushed through the door and slammed it in his wake. From the other side of the panel, she heard his muffled voice order, "Lock it."

She was aware of him waiting as she crossed the room and stood by the door, aware of his presence as she threw the deadbolt and slipped the chain into place. Once the door was secure, it was a long time before she heard the sound of his footsteps moving away.

She thought she heard him say *Be careful,* but that might just have been wishful thinking.

And why the hell was she wishing, anyway?

What was she wishing?

"Nothing good," she said aloud, thinking that the condo seemed empty all of a sudden. Thorne had filled it with his presence, with his warmth and anger.

And his visions.

What had he seen?

A shiver of cool air slid down her spine, as though the answer to that question had slipped through her brain and away so quickly she hadn't even noticed its passing.

"Doesn't matter," she told herself, and turned for the kitchen, intending to repack her first aid supplies and shoehorn them back into the small bathroom, which was one of the few things she didn't love about her condo. In a perfect world, the bathroom would be the size of her living room, and come complete with a whirlpool tub and double sink, just because. It would have—

She caught herself with the bottle in one hand and the glass in the other.

She hadn't even been aware of reaching for either.

Very, very carefully, Maya put the rum back on the breakfast bar, then set the glass beside it. Then she sat on the bar stool Thorne had used.

And closed her eyes.

They're called brown-outs, one of the rehab doctors had told her. *You're still up and moving around, but your brain isn't recording things properly. You aren't able to remember what you did, and you sure as hell aren't making rational decisions. Lots of alcoholics get them in the middle to late stages of the disease. With your allergy to alcohol dehydrogenase, you'll get them more easily, after just a few drinks, and they'll last longer. Needless to say, I wouldn't recommend you drink.*

"And I didn't," Maya said aloud. "I haven't been."

But a shiver worked its way down her spine and a nasty, hard ball of nerves gelled in her stomach.

Brown out.

Did that explain why she couldn't remember what had happened that night with Wexton Henkes? Could that explain the decisions she'd made—or at least the ones they said she'd made? But how could she have gotten to the point of browning out? She'd been on duty, in the middle of two big cases. She never would have taken a drink.

Yet just now, she'd nearly poured herself a few fingers of rum.

The lobby call button buzzed, making her jump, making her heart pound up into her throat. She thought about ignoring it, or maybe even calling security, but that would be giving in to the Mastermind and his fear games, so she forced herself to cross the room.

When she reached out to hit the Reply button, she was unnerved to see that she still had the highball glass in her hand.

She forced her voice steady when she said, "Hello?"

"It's me and Alissa." Cassie's voice was jarring with its cheerfulness. "Let us up. We come bearing take-out."

"Cass." Maya nearly slumped with relief. "Okay. Come on up." She buzzed them through, thought briefly about arming herself in case this was some sort of elaborate ruse, and decided that was overkill. But she checked the peephole just in case. When she saw her friends standing in the hallway, each carrying a big brown bag, she unlocked and unchained the door.

It wasn't until she'd opened the door and ushered them through that their visit struck her as odd.

The Mastermind had unleashed another crime wave against Bear Claw, yet the two remaining members of the Forensics Department were unpacking ribs and corn in her kitchen.

Something fishy was going on.

"Are you guys supposed to be protecting me or keeping me away from Henkes?" Maya asked quietly, and wasn't surprised when Alissa flushed.

Cassie had a better poker face, but after a moment, she sighed and said, "I told him you wouldn't buy it."

"The chief?" Maya assumed their boss still wanted her kept under wraps, wanted her kept as far away from Henkes as possible.

But Alissa shook her head. "No. The new guy. Thorne. He called us from the road and asked us to come out here. He sounded… strange." She shot Maya a glance. "Did something happen between you two that we—being your best friends and all—should know about?"

"Absolutely nothing," Maya said too quickly. Then she forced herself to slow it down when she said, "Unless you count the part where he refused Barnes's request to speak with me just before our only witness was gunned down."

"Mmm-hmm," Cassie said. She'd obviously already heard about Barnes's death and just as obviously wasn't buying Maya's explanation. "You sure that's all?"

"Positive," Maya said, this time making sure there was no room for doubt in her tone.

But as her friends started setting the table and the conversation shifted to a strained, slightly surface version of their usual casual chatter, Maya detected undercurrents she didn't understand, a subtext between her friends that she didn't get, didn't trust. What was going on here? What had happened back at the station that they weren't telling her about?

Had there been another message from the Mastermind? Another hint of where he planned to strike next? Or had they heard a rumor about the Internal Affairs inquiry, something they didn't want her to know about?

Those questions remained unanswered throughout the meal, while the armored warrior on the rum label looked down at her from the breakfast bar, winking as though he knew something Maya didn't.

The hell of it was, she feared he was right.

THORNE THOUGHT ABOUT DRIVING around the city and letting things percolate in his brain. Hell, he thought about heading north, back toward home, or at least toward the town he'd lived in for the past few years, home or not.

Instead, he drove to the Bear Claw PD, which was quiet with the late shift personnel and a few task force members struggling to pin down the latest series of threats. He waved to the uniformed officer manning the front desk, then headed straight for the basement. When he reached the Forensic Department offices, he breathed a sigh of relief that he was alone.

He needed a moment.

He sat at his desk amidst Maya's notes and scrubbed his hands together, one against the other in a washing motion, wishing it was that easy to erase the images that had flashed in his brain when he'd kissed her and the sexual buzz had turned into something else.

One moment he'd been giving in to the desire that had flared the moment he'd seen her again, the moment she'd tilted her chin and given him that go-to-hell look he couldn't resist. Stupid and ill-timed or not, the attraction was there and it wasn't fading as he had hoped. If anything, it was getting worse. He'd thought a kiss would blunt the feelings, but he'd been wrong about that, too. The heat, the desire, the need to possess had all reared up inside him, nearly too huge to manage.

But with them had come the half-formed images of things he'd done.

Things he had yet to do.

"Hey, what're you doing back here?" a man's voice said from the doorway. When Thorne snapped his head up and fought to re-assemble his professional shell, Tucker McDermott stepped into the office and leaned back against the wall in a habitual, contemplative pose Thorne recognized from the two task force meetings he'd attended since his arrival. The detective's eyes sharpened. "Something I should know about?"

"Nothing to do with the case," Thorne replied without really answering. "You got anything?"

"Maybe." McDermott looked at Thorne for a long minute before he asked, "What do you know about Wexton Henkes?"

That brought Thorne upright in his chair. "Not much." In fact, he'd actively avoided asking about Henkes. The chief's orders had been clear—keep Maya focused on something else. And though her actions seemed to suggest that she was a rational, thinking cop, he wasn't yet ready to go with her theory that Henkes was the Mastermind. It seemed like too much of a stretch, too convenient, given her recent history with the man.

He shifted in his chair and turned his full attention to the detective. "I know that Maya suspects that he's our guy, but it doesn't play for me. What little evidence she's got seems circumstantial at best."

"True enough." McDermott's expression remained pensive. "But I've been thinking..." He cursed softly. "Yeah, you're probably right." He shrugged. "Fact is, I like Maya. With Alissa involved, I'm anything but impartial, and the rest of the PD is on the other side of the fence because Henkes is a big supporter of the police charities. Maybe it's a good thing that you're here. We need someone who hasn't picked a side yet."

Thorne tamped down a bubble of cynical amusement.

He wasn't sure quite what he was when it came to Maya, but it wasn't impartial.

The detective said, "Maybe it's because of the Maya connection, but once I started looking at Henkes, a few things popped." He frowned. "There might be something there, but I don't want to go to the chief until I'm sure. Understand?"

Instincts prickling, Thorne gestured to the chair opposite him. "Sit. Tell me what you've found."

LATE THAT NIGHT, THE IMPROMPTU get-together broke up. Alissa went home near midnight, but Cassie crashed on Maya's couch, claiming she was too tired to drive home. Maya accepted the excuse, but she knew damn well that Cass was there as protection. Safety in numbers. She halfway expected Seth—Cassie's beau—to invite himself over.

But though she tried to go to bed mad, Maya slept deeply and awoke knowing that Thorne had been right to send her friends over.

She'd needed someone to stay with her. To babysit her, damn it.

Cassie left early, after passing on the news that Thorne would pick Maya up near nine. That gave Maya nearly two hours of brooding time after she dressed in the plainly cut navy sundress that was the only item of clothing that didn't aggravate her bruises. The black-and-blue marks on her ribs, knees and hip were a Technicolor reminder of the prison sniper incident, as was the fact that she couldn't drive herself to the station because she was under house arrest.

Frustration mounted at the realization that she lacked official sanction to do anything but sit on her butt and read a book while the case developed around her. Worse, Thorne was inviting her into the case with one hand while shutting her out with the other.

And he'd kissed her.

She felt a faint flush climb her face and touched her fingertips to her cheeks, then her lips. She'd managed to deflect Alissa and Cassie away from the subject, but hadn't succeeded in diverting her own thoughts. He'd crept into her dreams, which had been hot and unnerving, leaving her to wake throbbing and unfulfilled.

He was as much her weakness as alcohol. Or maybe they were intertwined, she wasn't sure anymore. But she knew she needed to armor herself against the pull, the temptation.

Her partying days were over, as were her days of giving in to impulse. She was older now, smarter. She wouldn't make a Dane-sized mistake again. She would have to figure out how to control herself around Thorne. She would have to discourage his attentions.

No matter how much part of her wanted them. Wanted him.

When he buzzed to be let up, she steeled herself against the sight of him. Or so she'd thought until she opened the door and saw him standing there wearing a button-down shirt open at the throat, paired with khakis and his heavy boots.

The air vibrated between them like a plucked string as he gave her long, practical dress a slow look that heated her blood with the memory of their kiss. But he said only, "Grab your stuff, we're late."

Maya forced herself to focus on the job. On the practicalities. "Since when does the chief keep to a schedule?" Parry was notorious for coming and going at odd hours, and always appearing when his cops least wanted him to overhear a gripe or admission of a mistake.

"We're not going to the station." Thorne held the door open, eyes daring her to go with him, daring her to refuse.

"Where, then?"

He waited until she was out in the hallway, waited until she had the door locked behind them before he said, "We have a meeting with Wexton Henkes. It's time to get to the bottom of what happened between you and him that night."

WHEN THE PHONE RANG IN his office, the Mastermind answered it without haste, knowing the plan was back on target. Barnes's death had been slightly premature, yes, but no matter.

It was fixable.

He lifted the handset. "Yes, Drew?"

"Coleridge and the woman are headed out. Want me to follow?"

"Don't bother. I'm ready for them." He paused and thought a moment before he said, "Meet me tonight on the Bear Claw Creek overpass. I have a new job for you."

"You got it. See you then."

When the line went dead, the Mastermind replaced the receiver, but kept his fingertips on the handset for a moment, thinking of the conversation and planning the next step.

The next death.

Chapter Nine

Maya should have been thrilled that Thorne had gotten them access to Henkes. She should have been relieved by the prospect of finally getting some answers.

Instead, she was nearly sick with worry.

Why was he doing this after he'd made such a point of diverting her away from Henkes? Was this on the chief's orders or his own initiative? And why?

But Thorne evaded her questions on the drive to the Henkes mansion in the cushy suburbs east of Bear Claw City, bringing another worry to the fore.

He'd said he didn't want her job, but the previous night Cassie and Alissa had made it clear they thought otherwise. What if the chief had offered him a deal?

Thorne already knew too much about her,

about the alcohol. What if this interview wasn't aimed at Henkes at all? Thorne could be looking for confirmation that she'd been drunk when she accosted Henkes.

Hell, Maya thought, *what if I was?*

Nerves sizzled through her as Thorne turned his car between the pillared gates of the Henkes estate and eased through the open gates. On either side of the bricked driveway, green lawns were clipped golf course short and misted by hidden spray heads. Sandy-toned rock walls curled around carefully planted flowerbeds and shrubs, then flowed up to the main house in an artful transition that looked stiff and artificial to her eye.

Thorne parked at the apex of the circular drive, right near the dozen or so marble steps that led up to the house. She sat for a moment, unmoving, staring up at the stone facade of the three-story house.

"Do you remember coming here that night?" he asked, voice carrying the soothing tones of a trained counselor.

A trained interrogator.

Of course, she wanted to say, *it was all planned. I already suspected that Henkes could be the Mastermind. I was trying to trick him into showing his hand.*

Instead, she shook her head. "No. I don't remember ever having been here."

She'd seen the crime scene photographs, the blood spatter from Henkes's bullet wound, and the corner of the marble-topped coffee table where she'd supposedly hit her head when she and Henkes had struggled for control of her gun. She'd driven past the huge house several times, trying to jump-start the memories.

But she didn't remember pulling into the driveway and knocking on the door as Wexton Henkes and his wife, Ilona, said she had done. She didn't remember anything until she'd awakened in the hospital three days later with a pounding headache the doctors had called a "natural response" to the head trauma she'd sustained.

She feared the headache—and the coma— had come from something else entirely. Something she wasn't ready to share with the others.

"You ready?" Thorne asked. He'd slid his shades up the bridge of his nose, leaving her to stare at the reflective surfaces and wonder what he was hoping to get out of this interview. Evidence against Henkes?

Or against her?

She took a deep breath to settle the nervous churn in her stomach. "Ready when you are."

They walked up the wide marble steps together, as though they were partners rather than…what? Friends? Adversaries? She didn't know anymore, maybe she'd never known, and the question unsettled her.

Thorne rang the doorbell, which tolled deep within the house. Moments later, the door swung open to reveal Wexton Henkes's wife, Ilona.

With her golden hair softened to pale by early strands of gray, and her athletic body thickened with her fifty-two years and a few too many dinners out, Mrs. Henkes should have seemed soft and motherly. Nurturing. But her eyes were hard and angry, her lips pressed together in a flat line. "I do not approve of this interview."

Thorne nodded. "I apologize for how awkward this must be for you. But as the chief explained, we have some questions for Mr. Henkes and we'd like to have Officer Cooper sit in on the meeting."

Ilona nodded stiffly. "She can come in, but only because William called and asked personally." She fired an angry look at Maya. "Kiernan isn't here. Otherwise you'd be headed back to your car this instant."

Mindful that she needed the woman's agreement for her to enter the premises—which were protected by a restraining order—Maya inclined her head but didn't comment. She and Ilona had met only once before, at the hospital when Kiernan's initial injuries had prompted Child Services to call the PD.

No, Maya realized as Ilona stepped back and stiffly gestured them into the house. They had met another time, at least according to Ilona's testimony. She had been there that night. She had been the one to let Maya into the house and lead her to the living room, where the struggle had occurred.

And she had been the one to call 911 when the shooting started.

The moment Maya stepped into the house, vague memories crowded around her, half-formed wisps of thought and cobweb images that might mean nothing, might mean something. She tried to grab on to them as she followed Thorne down an echoing marble-floored corridor, but the brown-tinged thoughtlets danced out of reach, leaving her frustrated and upset.

Then Ilona gestured them through a heavily paneled wooden door into a side room, and things got even stranger.

The moment Maya stepped inside, she knew she'd been in that room before. She sucked in a breath when she recognized the rows of books—mostly paperbacks—on the built-in shelves, and the ponderous, heavy-bellied mahogany desk on its ball-and-claw feet. She even recognized the chip in one claw, and vaguely remembered a voice telling her that Kiernan had done the damage with a remote-controlled car, and that instead of punishing the boy, Wexton had hunkered down on the floor and played with his son, seeing how much damage they could do with a lightweight radio-controlled dune buggy.

Memory or imagination? Maya wondered, though deep down inside, she damn well knew it was a memory.

She had been inside this room. Some-one—maybe even Wexton himself—had told her the story. But that didn't make any sense, Ilona had testified that she'd let Maya in the front door that night, and led her straight to the living room, where the struggle had later taken place.

According to the reports, Maya had never been in Wexton Henkes's study before. But she had been, she was sure of it.

Someone was lying. But who?

And why?

A cough drew her attention to Wexton Henkes, who sat behind the mahogany desk. In his early fifties, with his bald spot covered with a peewee hockey team ball cap and wearing a summer-weight sweater over an open-neck shirt, Henkes looked the picture of casual wealth. But his eyes were cool when he said, "Welcome to my home, Officer Coleridge." His expression chilled further when he shifted his attention to Maya. "Ms. Cooper."

The door opened again moments later to admit a younger, dark-haired man in a severely tailored navy suit and snugged-tight tie. He carried a briefcase and the slick assurance of a professional.

"Slade Pennington," Henkes said. "My lawyer. He'll be sitting in on this interview to make sure there are no…irregularities in the police procedure this time." His lips twisted on a parody of a smile, and when he gestured to a trio of chairs, his movement was stiff and pained.

Though more than three months had passed since the incident and the bandages were long gone, it was clear that the bullet wound high in the muscle of his right arm still bothered him.

Maya felt an unexpected pang of guilt.

They sat, and Thorne asked for and received permission to tape the interview. The lawyer, Pennington, sat quietly, his eyes fixed on Maya as though he were waiting for her to attack his client at any moment.

The intensity of his regard made her jittery.

"This interview has been requested by Chief William Parry, and may be terminated at any time by the interviewee, Wexton Henkes," Thorne said for the benefit of the tape. He then listed the date and time, and named each of the individuals in the room before he asked, "Where were you between the hours of eight and ten o'clock this past Monday morning?"

Henkes glanced at his lawyer, then back at Thorne, mid-brown eyes inscrutable. "I had a meeting at the Chuckwagon Ranch."

Adrenaline zapped through Maya, bringing her upright in her chair.

He'd been *where?*

"I thought this was about Ms. Cooper's inquiry." Henkes looked from Thorne to Maya, expression darkening. "I thought you had come to talk to me about the civil suit I'm considering filing against the PD. Harassment. Brutality. Defamation." His voice climbed. "I love my son, damn it! Don't you get that? I would never do anything to hurt him. Ask him yourself. *He had an accident!*"

Maya snapped, "That would be two accidents. Within a week. Accidents that he couldn't explain to the satisfaction of the ER doctors." Anger rose in her chest, nearly strangling her with its hot force. Though her own childhood had been safe, if constricting, she had met too many abuse victims in rehab and later through her work. She'd seen too many instances of abusers being protected by their families, by a society that preferred to look the other way.

She tried to make each abuse case

personal. If this one had gotten more personal than most, nobody needed to know why.

That, like so many other things, was in her past.

Henkes bristled and glared full at her. "Listen, you—"

"We're not here about your son," Thorne interrupted, his sharp tones cutting through the rising tension. "We're here about another case. And I need to know why you were at the ranch the other day. Where did you go, and who can verify your whereabouts the entire time you were on the premises?"

"I would like a moment to confer with my client in private," Pennington said. "You two can wait in the hall."

"No," Henkes countered. "I'll answer. I have nothing to hide—you can't pin that bomb threat on me. I was meeting with a group of investors who have expressed interest in purchasing my portion of the ranch." He rattled off the names and contact numbers of his associates, then smiled and leaned back in his chair, looking as though nobody could touch him and he damn well knew it.

Though Thorne fired off several follow-up questions, he wasn't able to shake the smug bastard.

Less than ten minutes into the interview, Pennington stood. "That will be all for now. Mr. Henkes has answered your questions fully and openly. Please feel free to contact me if you need to speak with my client again."

His tone suggested the request would be denied.

But as Ilona Henkes led Maya and Thorne to the front door and ushered them through it with a sour, hateful look, Wexton's voice followed them down the hall. "Wait one moment. I have a question for Officer Coleridge." He appeared in the doorway moments later with a nasty gleam in his pale eyes. "Haven't you ever wondered why she went after me in the first place? Don't you wonder why she's still after me?"

The blood froze in Maya's veins and the air fled from her lungs. A massive, leadlike weight pressed on her chest.

He didn't know. He couldn't know.

Could he?

"I take it you have a theory?" Thorne asked. His expression remained cool and closed.

"An observation, at the very least. My investigators looked into her background and found a few details I intend to pass on to your chief when I feel the time is right." The lawyer, Pennington, stood in the shadows behind his client, creating an odd juxtaposition of dark and light between the two men.

"Officer Cooper's past is her own business," Thorne said coolly. "I'm sure the chief already has all the relevant information."

He thought Henkes was talking about her drinking, Maya knew. He didn't realize there was more. She reached out and touched his sleeve. "We should go."

"You're right." Thorne turned away, but Henkes's voice called them back.

"Ask her about the accident, Officer Coleridge. Ask her about the dead boy. And then ask yourself whether that explains anything."

Thorne didn't react, didn't turn back or demand an explanation. He shot Maya a tight, angry glare and said, "Get in the car."

He had the engine revving before she dropped into the passenger's seat, had the Interceptor rolling before she got the door closed. She thought he would ask her about it once they reached the open road, where driving would give him an outlet for the restless, angry energy emanating from him.

Instead, he pulled over to the side of the road once they were clear of the Henkes mansion. He slammed on the brakes and turned to face her full-on. "Talk."

After a long, agonizing heartbeat, Maya opened her mouth, but nothing came out.

How could she talk about it? How could she explain?

She swallowed and forced the words past the knot in her throat. "I'm sorry. I should have told you sooner."

"Damn right." His expression was furious. Uncompromising. "Tell me now, so I know what we're dealing with." When she didn't respond right away, he said, "Damn it, Maya! If you've been withholding information that could make the PD look bad—"

"No, I wasn't!" She paused. "Not intentionally, anyway. I just didn't think it was relevant."

Thorne scowled. "Apparently, Henkes does. So spill it."

"I was married the day after my eighteenth birthday," Maya said, then paused, surprised when the pressure on her chest shifted to let her breathe more easily. Emboldened, she continued, "My parents approved the match—albeit reluctantly—because Dane was older and made a good living as a journalist. They thought he could control me the way they hadn't been able to. They figured once I was a married woman, I wouldn't be able to sneak out and party anymore."

"You told me about it," Thorne said unexpectedly. "That night at the academy, you told me about your marriage, how the only thing that changed was that the parties came home. You and your husband. His friends. One big bash. Then you started crying and passed out. You want to tell me the rest of the story now?"

Maya sucked in a breath. It didn't surprise her to learn that she'd spilled her guts that night. She talked freely when she was drunk.

But she was surprised by the burn of shame. Embarrassment. Grief.

The emotions still felt as sharp as they had eleven years earlier.

She swallowed and said, "Dane and I drank. A lot. We called it having fun, but in reality we were drinking to get drunk probably four, five nights a week." Unable to look at Thorne, she stared out the side window at a landscaped stand of trees, probably part of the Henkes estate. "One night, about eleven months into our marriage, Dane was supposed to pick up rum for me on the way home. I'd asked him that morning and called to remind him at lunch, but of course he forgot. I got mad and we had a fight, which was nothing new at that point. We really didn't have much in common." She had been bored and restless, annoyed with his absences and adrift without her parents ordering her around. "We were still bickering when we got in the car and headed for the liquor store. Dane had been drinking and I hadn't, because I was out of rum. But I let him drive, because it was no big deal to us. It had never been a problem before."

She swallowed, slammed anew with the knowledge that she could have prevented it, could have saved a life if she'd insisted on driving. *I'm fine,* Dane had snarled, *don't be such a nag.*

"I take it you hit someone?" Thorne said, drawing her eyes back to him.

She nodded, feeling the touch of his gaze as though it was a physical force. "It was a rainy Saturday night in May. Dane took the highway off-ramp too fast, lost control and hit a car carrying four high school kids on their way to the prom. Our car stayed on the ramp, but we pushed the other car through the rail and over. It flipped and fell…" Her eyes filled with tears as the rage of grief and horror rose up to swamp her again, as fresh as it had been that night. "I knew the kids. They were two years behind me in school. Luce and Krista were in the drama club. Jason played on the football team. They wound up with broken bones. Internal injuries. Jason spent a month in the hospital, learning how to walk again. No NFL for him."

"And the fourth victim?"

Maya closed her eyes. "He died."

"What was his name?"

She opened her eyes and looked at Thorne, saw the knowledge in his eyes. "Kiernan. His name was Kiernan. And before you ask me, yes, that was the first thing I thought of when Child Services called me on Kiernan Henkes. There's even some resemblance— they're both athletic, both have rusty blond hair and freckles." She twisted her fingers together in her lap. "That's what Henkes meant. He's implying that I went after him because saving his Kiernan from danger helped me feel like I was atoning for the other Kiernan's death. Depending on how good his investigator is, he could very well tell the inquiry board that I took a drink that night because I couldn't handle the memories, that I was drunk when I attacked him."

"Were you?"

She wanted to deny it, to snap at Thorne for even asking the question, but she couldn't. All she could do was stare at her hands. "God help me, I don't know."

Silence thundered in the small space as she waited for his response, for the scorn and the accusations she deserved.

Instead, after a long moment he cursed under his breath, shifted the transmission back into Drive and gunned the Interceptor into a tight U-turn that headed them back toward the city.

She hung on tightly to the door handle. "Where are we going?"

"To the hospital," he grated. A muscle worked at the corner of his jaw. "We're going to find out whether you were drunk that night."

Maya's fingers tightened their grip. "And if I was?"

He glanced at her, expression unreadable. "Then we'll deal with it."

The promise was scant comfort.

ONCE THEY REACHED the Hawthorne Hospital Emergency Room, Thorne commandeered an intern and showed his badge. When he had the kid's attention, he said, "Do you remember a shooting about three months ago?"

The young man's eyebrows drew together. "We get a few of those a week. Can you give me deets?"

Maya said, "Two victims—a fifty-something-year-old man shot in the arm, and a thirtyish woman, unconscious from a blow to the head." Her voice was subdued, her skin pale, but Thorne buried the surge of concern.

She'd lied to him and to her chief, if not actively, then by omission. She should have disclosed the connection to the other Kiernan the moment she regained consciousness, and she should have checked the hospital records months ago.

The fact that she hadn't set off warning bells for Thorne.

The intern's eyes lit. "You mean when the cop shot Wexton Henkes? I heard about that. That happened just before I started here, but I heard—"

"Can you direct us to the admitting doctor, please?" Thorne interrupted, fighting to keep the snarl out of his voice.

The kid fell back a step. "Um, sure. Wait right here."

Within five minutes, they had the third-year resident who'd worked on Maya, and they had her chart.

But they didn't have the information they needed.

Dr. Rashid, a lovely, dark-haired, dark-skinned woman, shook her head. "I'm sorry, Officers. The test wasn't performed at the time of admission."

Aware of Maya standing at his side, pale and drawn, Thorne said, "Wouldn't it be standard procedure to take a blood alcohol level when an unconscious patient was admitted with reports of irrational and violent behavior?"

"Normally, yes," the doctor agreed, "and

I drew blood for the examination. But there is no evidence that the test was ever run. I'm sorry. I don't remember why the order was canceled. It was…hectic that night."

Thorne's suspicions prickled. "Did someone cancel the order? A cop, maybe?"

"I don't remember, and there's no note. I'm sorry." But the doctor's eyes slid away from them. "If there's nothing else, I have patients to see."

"Do you still have the blood samples in storage?" Maya asked, voice stronger than he would have expected.

Dr. Rashid shook her head. "They wouldn't do you any good now. Decomposing blood generates alcohol. Even with anti-clotting agents, preservatives and frozen storage, the sample would likely show positive for alcohol, regardless of the original levels."

Maya's shoulders slumped. "Right. I knew that."

The doctor excused herself and left them alone in the treatment room.

"You okay?" Thorne asked, though it was damn clear she wasn't even close to being okay. Her skin was so pale it was nearly translucent, except where it showed the duskiness of angry bruises along her arms. Her eyes were shadowed and sad, and she looked small, tinier than his mental image of her, and fragile with it.

"I'll be fine," she said, stressing the last word as though trying to convince herself of the fact. "It's just…" She blew out a breath. "I wasn't sure I wanted to know the answer before. But now it's a huge disappointment to realize the damn test was never run."

"And a huge question mark as to why it wasn't?"

She frowned. "I hope you're not implying that I had anything to do with that decision."

"You were unconscious. You had no say in the matter, which leads me to wonder who did." Thorne considered the possibilities. "And why didn't whoever it was want your levels tested? It doesn't make any sense."

"Which probably means it's just one of those random things. An oversight." She gestured to the door. "Come on. We need to keep looking."

But when she reached for the doorknob, he saw that her fingers were trembling. The sight of that fine tremor, that fragility, reached inside him and squeezed his heart.

The night before he hadn't intended to kiss her. God knows he wasn't looking to start something complicated with a coworker in Bear Claw when he'd just ended something messy with one back home. But even knowing that, he'd kissed her and been lost.

He touched the small of her back to guide her out of the ER curtain room. "Come on, we've got to talk." He hadn't braced himself against he flash of touching her, and was surprised when it didn't come, when he felt only the warmth of her clothing and the firm muscles beneath.

She followed his lead, but said, "Talk about what?"

He didn't answer until they were outside the hospital, out in the fresh air of a sunny, innocent-seeming summer day. Needing to burn off the energy zipping along beneath his skin, he turned her toward a large park the hospital maintained for its patients and their families, for those times that called for a bit of fresh air and greenery, a bit of privacy.

Feeling as though he was being guided from outside himself, Thorne led her down a brick pathway, into a mazelike area where towering hedges screened them from the hospital and the other walkers. At the center of the maze, they found a small doorway marked simply Meditation.

Somehow, he'd known it would be there.

He knocked, and when nobody answered, pushed through the door into a small space bounded by hedges. A sandstone bench sat beneath a shade tree within, and the door could be locked from the inside, protecting privacy for meditation.

Or conversation.

He gestured to the bench set beneath a shade tree. "Sit."

"I'll stand, thank you just the same." Maya tilted her chin up as though bracing for a blow.

"Fine. I'll sit." Thorne suited action to words, then waited until she joined him on the bench, which was short enough that their knees touched.

He felt only human warmth at the contact, and wondered why the flashes had threatened to break through before, but not now. Had he imagined them in the first place?

Or was something else going on?

Aware of Maya watching him with

shadowed, troubled eyes, Thorne tabled that question and shifted to face her more fully. "I think we're working at cross-purposes. We're getting in each other's way when we could be working together. We need to stop doing that and focus on what's important."

Though he hadn't been aware of making the decision, it sounded right. It *felt* right.

She leaned away. "And what do you consider important? Redecorating my office?"

"I told you I'm not interested in your job," he said, though that wasn't entirely true. "I'm saying we need to figure out what happened to you that night. I think you're right. I think there might be a connection between the Mastermind and what happened at the Henkes mansion."

Her eyes blanked. "You believe me? You think Henkes could be our guy?"

"I'm not going that far, but your suspension has acted to destabilize the Bear Claw PD, which can only benefit the Mastermind's plan." Thorne thought it through aloud. "Drew Wilson could be the Mastermind, not another of his lackeys. It would work on a couple of levels—Wilson has police training and ex-plosives experience through the military."

"He's not smart enough." Maya stood and began to pace the small space in a move that reminded Thorne of himself. "His coworkers all said he was only as smart as he needed to be. That doesn't fit the Mastermind's profile."

"Unless he played dumb at the prison," Thorne said. The restless energy of her pacing echoed inside him, sparking the heat of frustration, inaction. He stood and intercepted her, forcing her to stop before she bumped square into him. "I'm serious, Maya. I want us to share our information and work together. For real this time." He held out his hand to her. "What do you say? Partners?"

After a long, motionless moment, she nodded. "Okay. No more secrets between us."

Before he could argue that wasn't what he'd said or meant, she took his hand.

The flash ripped through him, almost fully formed now. It showed him the future.

A gunshot. Blood. A scream.

And his own finger on the trigger as he killed again.

Chapter Ten

Thorne flinched and tried to pull away from their handclasp, but this time Maya didn't let him go. She held on tight and followed him when he backed across the small clearing. His broad shoulders bumped up against the tall hedge and his face went white as chalk.

"What do you see?" she said, keeping her voice low and calm.

Thorne's grip went lax in hers and a shudder rolled through his body. But his voice was tinged with bleak, black humor when he said, "Trust me. You don't want to know about the things I see."

She let her hands fall away, unaccountably disappointed. "In other words, that whole 'full disclosure, let's be partners' speech was a crock." She stepped back. "You don't trust me and I don't trust you. Why are we bothering?"

Hollow frustration beat within her, the knowledge that she didn't have anyone on her side, and that working with Thorne was complicating more than it was helping. Maybe it was time to walk, time to go it alone.

But as she watched him pace, watched the lean strength of him, the leashed anger that vibrated through his body and sent an answering quiver through hers, she realized that she might not be able to walk away. He drew her just as surely as he'd done back in their academy days, though for different reasons. Back then, he'd been the good-time guy, the partier so like the ex-husband—and the part of herself—that she'd been trying to outrun. Now, he was dark and unhappy, maybe even a little violent. And that darkness drew her.

Worse, he could be her only hope at this point. She needed somebody on her side at a time when even Cassie and Alissa couldn't help her.

So she sat on the bench, feeling the cold of the stone seep through the fabric of her sundress. "You want honesty and full disclosure? Fine. You've got it. But you owe me the same in return."

The decision surged in her gut like nausea, like fear, but what was her other option?

There wasn't one. Period.

Knowing it, hating it, she said, "You know the rum bottle in the cabinet? That was the one Dane and I bought the night we got in the accident. The night we killed Kiernan Surhoff. I kept it as a symbol." As penance. "The seal has been unbroken for eleven years." She reached up with both hands and unfastened the clasp of her charm necklace. When the chain fell free, she pulled one end up and away, so the five charms dropped into her palm. "When I was released from observation at the hospital, I checked the cabinet first. I think I already knew that I'd find the bottle open."

She flicked her wrist and tossed the charms into the thick, green hedge surrounding the meditation area.

They glittered in the sunlight, then were gone, leaving an aching void deep in her soul. A sense of loss.

Of failure.

"I bought a charm for each year I was sober," she said, though he hadn't asked. "After the night you and I—the night we spent together, I tossed the six charms I wore back then and started collecting a new set." She stared into the hedge. "I don't know if I can start over again."

But she had to. What other choice was there?

When he didn't say anything, didn't move, she continued, "I'd like to think there's another explanation, but it makes too much sense. I took it personally when Kiernan Henkes was hurt. Maybe too personally, I don't know. The whole case bothered me—how neither the boy nor his mother could explain the injuries, and how Henkes was evasive on questioning. Even the chief agreed it was strange."

Thorne glanced at the edge of the brick walkway, where one of the fallen charms lay abandoned. "Do you remember opening the bottle?"

She shook her head. "No. I don't."

"Do you remember drinking the night we were together?"

"I don't know what that—" She broke off, then a ball of excitement tightened in her chest as she answered, "Yes. I remember you pouring the whiskey. I remember how it smelled, how it looked in the glass. I remember telling you I was sober."

"And I pushed you," he said, eyes dark. "For what it's worth, I'm sorry. Back then, I was threatened by people who didn't drink, because I drank so damn much. I think I wanted…hell, I don't know what I wanted, but I'm sorry. I wish things had happened differently that night."

The simple sincerity touched her, bringing a tight knot to her throat. She swallowed to clear the emotion. "We both made mistakes. We both survived. But the important thing right now is that you're right. I remember that night. But I don't remember drinking the night I went after Henkes. The last thing I remember is…" She thought back. "I remember coming home from the hospital. I'd been by to see Kiernan, but his father wouldn't let me in the room. He said Kiernan was sleeping, and when I insisted, he told me to come back with a warrant. I hated his smug attitude and his lawyer, and I was ticked that the chief didn't want to prosecute his own fishing buddy. I came home and—" She held up her hands. "That's it. Nothing else until I woke up in that hospital room."

Thorne's expression grew grim. "Would the chief have tried to cover for you if he thought you were drunk?"

"Never. Not in a million years. He's a good cop, smart and by-the-book."

"What about your friends?"

Though her first instinct was to go on the defensive, Maya waited a beat, then went with honesty. "Alissa and Cassie don't know much about my... history with alcohol. They know I don't drink, but they think it's because I was married to an alcoholic. And besides, they wouldn't interfere with a case. Not even for me." She dropped her face into her hands. "Which leaves us exactly nowhere, unless..." She trailed off as a thought occurred to her, one that had been skirting the edges of her mind for days. She'd pushed off the temptation as impractical. Dangerous.

But now it might be their only option.

She took a deep breath. "I want you to regress me. I did it before, with Alissa during the Canyon Kidnapping case. It helped." Perhaps they hadn't gotten the information they'd expected, but it had helped, nonetheless.

Only now Maya wouldn't be the one in control.

Thorne would.

She swallowed and continued, "If the memories are in there, you'll be able to get them out. We need to know what happened at the Henkes mansion, and we need to know now."

But instead of jumping at the chance to get inside her head, Thorne scowled. "You're telling me that of all the professionals you worked with at the hospital or through the department, none of them hypnotized you after the Henkes incident, trying to find the memories?"

Maya jammed her hands in the pockets of her sundress and hunched her shoulders. "What does that matter?"

"Did they?" he persisted.

Frustration clamped a hot, angry vise around her chest. "They didn't get anything. Not a damn thing."

"Then what makes you think I would get something when the others couldn't?"

"Because..." Maya faltered, thinking, *because I feel like you know me better than those others.* "You said it yourself—the flashes are starting to break through the barriers you've built. Damn it, you had one just now—don't tell me you didn't. What if they're trying to tell you something important? What if they're trying to show you something that would help us solve the case?" Ignoring his suddenly closed expression, she stood and took a step toward him. "I know you don't want the visions. I'm not even sure I believe that they're real. But if they can help...don't you owe it to the innocent victims to try?"

Thorne cursed under his breath. "Christ, not you, too."

"What does that mean?"

"It means that I'm not a damn side show, or some jackass psychic detective. You can't give me a scarf and get a name in return— the stories were exaggerated."

Hearing the raw emotion in his voice, Maya took a step toward him, until they were close enough to touch. "Back at the academy, they said you could see the future."

It wasn't quite a statement, wasn't quite a question.

She expected him to shrug it off. Instead, he stayed still and locked eyes with her. "Some days I thought I could. Other days I convinced myself that the doctors were right, that it was just flashbacks from the drugs, or delusions from post-traumatic stress. But all that changed the night we spent together."

THORNE SAW THE SHOCK IN her eyes and wondered why the hell he was telling her this when it would serve nothing for the current case.

"How so?" she asked, her voice sounding suddenly small.

He wanted to pace, he wanted to move, hell, he wanted to be somewhere else entirely. But instead of running away, as he had done too many times before, he jammed his hands in his pockets and said, "That night you told me about your husband, about the drinking. You didn't tell me about the accident, but you talked about rehab and how hard you fought to get clean after you left him. And I—" He cursed. "I don't know. Maybe I was getting ready to see it on my own and you tipped the balance. It shook me to realize that all ninety-eight-pounds-wet of you was tougher than me. We'd both had bad times, and we both knew what it was like to wake up thinking about nothing more than that first drink. But you'd found your way out. I hadn't." He glanced at his hands, saw that they were balled into fists, and consciously uncurled them and pressed them flat against his upper thighs. "When you passed out, I stayed up and watched you sleep. And I decided to make some changes."

Her eyes darkened. "Because of me?"

"No. Because of me. You were the catalyst, though, and I owe you for that." Which was why he was going to do his damnedest to see that she kept her position in Bear Claw, he realized suddenly. He couldn't take her job. He wouldn't. Feeling a weight lift off his chest, he spread his hands away from his body. "I stopped drinking and took up meditation and martial arts. I figured out the connection between my mind and body, and how to block the flow. I tuned the visions out." He shrugged. "Or maybe I'm kidding myself about that. Maybe my brain finally healed enough that I stopped having the visions."

"You don't believe that."

He shook his head. "No. Because if that was the case, why are they coming back now?" He feared he already knew the answer.

They were coming back because of her.

Getting to know her had given him the strength and the resolution to fight off the flashes. Now, being around her was letting them break free. But why?

"What are they showing you now?" she asked again, persisting when he didn't want to see, just like Tabitha had.

Resentment welled up. She didn't understand what the flashes did to him. What they showed him. "I'm not seeing a damn thing right now and I'd like to keep it that way. I told you, I'm not some sort of a sideshow fr—"

In one smooth move, she leaned down and framed his face in her hands. "What do you see now?"

And she kissed him.

Colors exploded in his brain, hues that matched the rocketing sensations as he took Maya in his arms and crushed her to his chest, trying to burn away the images of blood with the heat of contact. Of connection.

Though he suspected she'd kissed him to provoke a flash, and thought he might damn her for it later, at that moment he could only ride the wave of heat that surround him. Pounded him. The sounds of an imagined gunshot and a woman's ghostly scream were blotted out by the roar of blood through his veins, the thunder of his heartbeat echoing inside his head.

Then, in an instant, the violence of the images became something else entirely.

Sex.

"What do you see?" she whispered, returning him to the moment, to the feel of the woman in his arms, the power of a connection he hadn't wanted, but now didn't want to escape.

"I see you," he said before his brain jammed on the images of Maya's creamy skin bared beneath her sundress, her legs wrapped around his waist as he leaned back against the spreading shade tree that was just a few steps away. "I see us."

It was too much too soon, he knew. They weren't ready for that level of intimacy. Hell, *he* wasn't ready, wasn't sure he'd ever be, especially with the half-formed visions of what was to come.

What he'd vowed not to let happen.

Knowing it, he pressed a soft, undemanding kiss to her lips, one intended to please without promising, to excite without unleashing the desires he held in check.

At least that was his intention. But in the moment that their lips touched, the heat reached up and grabbed him, pulled him into the images, into the sensations that crashed within his body, a combination of what was and what might be. He deepened the kiss almost unintentionally, slanting his mouth across hers and parting his lips, finding hers open in return.

Their tongues touched and paused, then touched again with more pressure, more confidence as the blood beat within his head, within his heart.

Yes, it seemed to say, *this is right. This is good. This is what you need.*

But was it what *she* needed?

MAYA FELT THE CHANGE IN HIM, felt the tension sneak back in, felt him withdraw the part of himself he'd given up during that first moment, when she'd kissed him in an effort to force honesty and had found heat instead.

Worse, she'd found want. Desire. A readiness to chuck caution and go with the sensations, which was so totally foreign to her makeup that she didn't know how to handle the urge. Because of it, she was almost relieved when he pulled away. One part of her brain howled for her to keep going, to reach for him, twine herself around him again and deal with the aftermath later, when things were already done.

But another part of her, the part that remembered brown-outs and angry words, that part wasn't sure.

"You asked me what I saw." His eyes were nearly black with desire and maybe something more, sending a shiver through her midsection, a mixture of fear and want. His voice roughened when he said, "I saw us making love. Here. Now. The sun was shining and a bird sang in the tree above us." He swallowed hard. "I know that's what I want, rationality be damned. I want us to be together. Not forever, but for right now. I need to know it's right for you, too."

The unexpected question startled her, as did the vulnerability in his eyes. He held out a hand to her, making her realize that he'd stepped back away from her, giving her room.

Giving her a choice.

What did she want? What was right for her?

As she stood there in the sun-dappled

courtyard and a small bird fluttered down to alight in the branches overhead, she realized the two questions might not have the same answer. She didn't know what was right for her, not at this point in her life. Her job was up in the air, her future on the line. But she damn well knew what she wanted. She wanted the man in front of her. The man watching her with dark, searching eyes. The man whose taste lingered on her tongue, whose masculine scent danced in her nostrils as the bird on the branch above her began to sing.

There it was then, Maya thought, being brutally honest with herself. This might not be what was right for her, but it was what she wanted. She wanted Thorne, wanted to take him deep inside her and figure out the rest later. *Not forever,* he'd said, and she would have to accept that.

She took a step toward him, then another, closing the distance until the heat from his body prickled across her skin. "This is right for me. Maybe it won't be tomorrow or next week, but it's right for me now. I'm a big girl. I know what I'm getting into."

He drew breath as if to argue, but she was

done with talking, done with circling around the baldest of facts. They had desire between them. Chemistry. They were mature, consenting adults. She didn't need the promise of forever anymore.

She didn't *want* forever. She wanted right now, then goodbye, so they could go on with their separate lives. He was coming out of a relationship and she wasn't looking for one, certainly not with a man like him.

But they could have the moment they should have had five years earlier.

When a shiver of something tightened her shoulders, prescience perhaps, she touched his chest with her fingertips, felt the thump of his heartbeat, and slid her hands up to link them behind his neck, so the two of them were pressed chest-to-chest, thigh-to-thigh. "I want this."

As though an invisible rubber band had snapped, the tension went out of Thorne. He dropped his forehead to hers, and touched his hands to her hips, caressing rather than gripping. "Heaven help me, so do I."

They kissed, meeting halfway as equals in desire, in decision. The heat of the dappled sunlight, the sound of the birdsong and the light fragrance of warm earth and growing things rose up to surround them, sending an uncharacteristic ache through Maya's heart.

She couldn't afford to let this be about romance. That sort of thing didn't work for her. This was about the physical, nothing more. So she focused on the sensations, the slide of heat and flesh and the taste of him when she unbuttoned the top of his shirt and pressed a kiss to his collarbone, to the hollow of his throat.

She had wanted this since the first moment she'd seen him in the parking lot above the Chuckwagon Ranch. She'd wanted this even before, back when they'd been in the academy and she hadn't wanted anyone, least of all herself.

"Maya," he said, whispering her name once, and then again as though it was the answer to a question she hadn't asked.

He brushed a kiss against the side of her neck and her world tilted, then shifted on its axis. There was nothing left in her conscious mind except him, the taste of him, the smell of him, the feel of him beneath her fingers as she fumbled with the rest of his shirt buttons, then reached beneath to touch the ribbed planes of his torso, the tight skin and taut muscles across his sides and back, as she removed the material completely.

This wasn't about the case anymore, wasn't about her history with Dane, or about her fears that she might not have a job anymore, might not have the future she'd planned.

This was about her. About them.

About the moment.

She murmured pleasure when his stroking hands clamped on her waist and boosted her up so their mouths were aligned. It seemed the most natural thing in the world to part her legs and wrap them around his waist, allowing her skirt to fall away. She felt the naughty chafe as her inner thighs slid across the material of his pants, then on to the bare skin above.

Thorne growled deep in his throat and slid his warm hands down to support her, cupping her bottom where her panties gave way to skin.

She was wet and hot and wanting at the apex of her thighs, where her body was aligned with his through the frustrating layers of clothing. She moved against him, with him, wanting more, wanting it all.

As though in synchrony with her wishes, he

turned and bent low to deposit her on the bench while he stepped away. Their eyes never broke contact as she shimmied out of her panties and he undid his belt and zipper, and shoved his pants down far enough to free himself.

A small part of her panicked, shouting, *What the hell are you doing? This is crazy! Insane! Irresponsible! What are you getting yourself into?*

But she shoved the voice aside as she watched him fumble for his wallet, for the single condom that rested in his billfold. When he rejoined her near the bench, she didn't notice the hard coolness of the stone beneath her, or the hard rasp of the tree at her back. She barely comprehended the warmth of the sun or the final trill the bird gave before it fluttered away.

Stuck in the moment, in the *now,* she only noticed him, noticed the play of shadow and light across the skin bared by his open shirt, across the proud jut of his manhood as he knelt before her and aligned his body to hers.

Maya didn't try to analyze the experience, didn't bother to try to figure the future. She let her head fall back, baring her throat to his kisses, and let her legs spread wide, opening herself to him, inviting him into her body, but not her heart. Not this time. She was old enough and smart enough to protect that part of herself.

Or so she hoped.

He entered her with a whisper. Her name. His. It didn't matter who said the words, only that they were said, binding the two of them together in that first moment of joining, when her flesh clenched tight to reject him, then softened to let him inside.

Then he paused, waiting.

Maya lifted her head and met his eyes, which were hazel and mismatched, and for the first time since she'd known him, clear of shadows. They looked at each other for a long moment, asking and answering unanswerable questions, until she smiled and so did he, and they met halfway for a kiss. "What do you see?" she asked against his lips.

"I see you," he said in return and began to move within her. To move with her.

Desire tightened, flooding her with a new, pounding need that had been banked to a warm glow only moments before. She tangled her fingers in his shirt, holding him closer, binding them as their bodies pistoned together and apart, together and apart.

What had begun as gentle lovemaking morphed into a frantic scramble, a sweaty, straining union with only one possible endpoint.

Climax. Explosion.

When the moment came, Maya clamped her legs around his hips and cried out, "Thorne!" She didn't care who heard her, whether it was the birds or other passersby. The naughty thrill of being outdoors, of being in public crested alongside the physical release, pummeling her with pleasure.

"Maya." He said her name on a groan and followed her over, shuddering with the force of his own release, clamped in a vise of tension that rocketed through his body until he went limp and collapsed against her, pressing her into the bench and the tree and all the external things that were once again present, but didn't yet mean a damn thing to her.

The only thing that meant anything in that moment was the good, solid weight of Thorne's body against her and the rise and fall of his chest in tandem with her breaths. They could think about the other things later.

Except that *later* came in mere moments, when Thorne's phone chimed from the side pocket of his half-mast pants.

The rude interruption chilled Maya, as did that same little voice she'd ignored moments earlier, which now said, *What the hell have I done?*

"Ignore it," he said, the words breezing against the side of her neck, where he'd pressed his bowed head in the aftermath.

For a moment she thought he was talking about the voice. Then she realized the phone was still ringing. As gently as she could, she levered him away, needing the distance as reality sank in and she realized they hadn't solved anything.

No, they'd complicated everything instead.

"You should answer it," she said, leaning back, unlocking her thighs from his hips and tucking her skirt between them, so she was almost returned to pre-sex modesty, save for her panties, which lay on the brick walkway beneath them. "It might be something about the case."

His eyes clouded, then cleared with understanding a moment before his expression blanked to neutral. "Oh. So that's how it's going to be." He stood and refastened his pants with quick, businesslike movements that held the edge of anger.

"I don't know what you're talking about." She stood and stepped into her panties as deftly as she could, given that she snagged one foot in the elastic. With her clothing restored—if not her dignity—she nodded and said, "Answer it. We can talk about this later. Or not. Your call."

She held her breath for a beat after the offer, part of her hoping he would insist on a conversation.

Instead, he nodded distractedly and flipped open the phone. "This is Coleridge." He listened for a minute, face growing grimmer by the second. He hung up without another word.

"Problem?" she asked.

"The chief wants us at the hockey rink. There's been an explosion."

Chapter Eleven

Thorne saw Maya freeze. The whole scene stilled, until he swore he could pick out each individual pollen mote on the summer air, each beam of sunlight that filtered down to gleam on the rich, dark hair he had touched only moments before as he'd poured himself into her.

Moments before, when innocents had been dying at the Mastermind's hands.

"How many casualties?" she asked.

"Two dead." He wanted to reach for her, to support her, but he didn't dare because he wanted it too much. So instead, he worked on fastening the buttons of his shirt, staring down at them so he wouldn't have to see her face when he said, "One maintenance worker and one civilian, a chaperone on a children's field trip."

She swore. "Were the children hurt? Was there any warning, any—"

"We won't know until we get there," he interrupted, body now thrumming with the need to get to the scene, to get back to work.

To get away from this small, sheltered nook where he'd done what he'd promised himself he wouldn't. He'd made lo—been intimate with Maya.

He knew better, damn it.

As he jammed his shirt into his waistband and waved her out of the clearing, Thorne had to admit to himself that knowing better hadn't stopped him, and he would have to deal with the consequences. He'd have to make sure she understood this wasn't going anywhere, couldn't go anywhere.

But as he followed her from the clearing, he paused by the gate, turned back and looked at the spreading shade tree. The bird had returned, or maybe another one had dropped in. The little scrap of wing and feather tilted back its head and sang, just as it had done in his vision.

I saw us making love, he'd said. *The sun was shining and a bird sang in the tree above us.*

A faint shiver touched his skin. Had it been an educated guess dressed in poetry, or a premonition? Had the visions truly returned?

It was a lucky guess, his brain argued, while his heart said, *it was prescience.*

It didn't matter, he told himself. It had happened and he'd have to deal with it.

They both would.

MAYA WAS FURIOUS WITH HERSELF by the time they reached the hockey rink. The site was on her suspect list—it was part-owned by Wexton Henkes—but she hadn't followed up on it. She'd allowed herself to be distracted by other details. By Thorne.

And two innocents had paid the price.

Worse, as the reports filtered in over Thorne's radio and cell phone, it became clear that children had been injured, as well. The bomb had detonated in a maintenance area, near the controls governing the ice surface. A nearby rink employee had been killed instantly, a twenty-two-year-old named Howie who'd just graduated from Bear Claw College and had been headed to grad school in the fall. The force of the blast had blown out a nearby wall, sending shrapnel into a group of kids who'd been waiting for their turn on the ice.

Stacy Littleton, mother of two, had also been killed. Four children were badly injured, and maybe a dozen others had suffered minor lacerations, bumps and bruises.

When they reached the scene, Maya was out before Thorne had the Interceptor parked. She was aware of him at her side as she jogged toward the Bear Claw College ice rink, which was a low, wide building made of preformed concrete slabs dressed up with cement swirls in the shapes of figure skaters and hockey players. The building itself appeared undamaged from the outside, but fire trucks, ambulances and hustling rescue personnel jammed the sidewalk near the main entrance, telling of the destruction within.

Maya pushed through, aware that Thorne waved off several cops who advanced, maybe to talk to her, more likely to tell her she had no place on the scene.

Maybe she didn't have an official role, but she damn sure had a moral role, one that became all too apparent when she stepped inside the main lobby and heard the children's cries. Saw the tears and the blood.

She should have stopped this, should have stopped *him.*

Instead, she had been with Thorne, wasting time and energy, splitting their resources and focus.

He'd been right in the first place. They needed to stop working at cross-purposes and catch this bastard once and for all.

More importantly, they needed to stop being distracted by each other.

Ten kids, ranging in age from six to maybe twelve, huddled against the far wall, being tended by a trio of paramedics. The rescue workers' faces wore professional calm tinged with an undertone of sadness. Of anger.

Maya felt that same anger gutter within her. She didn't go to the children. She didn't have that right, and it wouldn't solve a damn thing. Instead, she glanced toward the main doors, one of which hung ajar on its hinges. Emergency lights lit the scene, indicating that the blast had knocked out the main power. A faint trail of smoke worked its way along the ceiling, and a crackle of radio traffic picked up on Thorne's portable told that the bomb squad was already at work.

She jerked her head toward the doors. "I need to get in there."

Thorne nodded. "Wait here. I'll make sure the scene is secure."

When he was gone, Maya moved off to the side of the lobby and leaned on the wall near an intersecting hallway that led to the equipment shop. Her brain vibrated with the noise, a combination of young and old voices, sirens and sobs.

The reality of it echoed through her. She could have stopped this. She *should* have stopped it.

She should have shot Henkes dead that night. Deep down inside, she knew that truth. Nobody else might believe her, but the proof would have been there for all to see.

In the wake of his death, the attacks would have stopped.

Surely, that would have been proof enough?

"Hssst!"

Maya's head snapped up at the whisper. She turned toward the hallway, but could make out little in the dimness. "Who's there?"

"I need to talk to you, but they can't see." The voice was young and male, and cracked with stress. "Come on. Over here!"

Adrenaline was a quick punch in her gut when she recognized the voice. "Kiernan?"

"Quick, before they see us talking!"

Maya hesitated and glanced from the main door, where Thorne stood talking to the chief, to the deserted hallway, which was lit only by dim emergency lights. She saw the silhouette of a young man leaning on a single crutch.

Wexton's son. The boy whose injuries had never been adequately explained, but who insisted his father hadn't knocked him around.

Making a quick decision, she stepped through the open arch into the darkened hallway. "What are you doing here?"

The figure backed away, further into the shadows, sending a skitter of nerves along her skin. She reached behind her back to loosen the strap on her mid-back holster, only to find the weapon gone.

It, like her badge, rested on a locked shelf in the chief's office.

Defenseless, she held her hands away

from her sides and kept her weight balanced on the balls of her feet as she advanced down the hallway, poised to fight or flee as necessary.

"You said you had something to tell me." She pitched her voice low and soothing, though a sense of danger pulsed along her nerve endings like fire. "Is it about your father?"

She was close enough now to see Kiernan's wide eyes and the nervous way his fingers picked at the foam rubber covering the hand grip of his single crutch. The last time she remembered seeing the twelve-year-old boy in person, he'd been in the hospital, unconscious from the "accident" that had left him with a badly broken leg and a large knot on the back of his head.

She remembered looking down at him and feeling the crushing weight of failure. It had been her decision to return the boy to his family after he'd insisted that the bone bruise on his wrist had been an accident, that he'd fallen down playing, nothing more. It had been her decision to give in to the chief's pressure not to prosecute Wexton Henkes.

Now, she looked at the boy, at the hint of

desperation in his eyes and the way his leg stuck out awkwardly to one side in its brace, and felt her heart clutch in her chest.

Her decision. Her failure.

"I know I'm not supposed to talk to you." His eyes darted from her to the lobby and back. "But my mom's not here and I…" He blew out a breath and tried again. "Before, in the hospital, you asked me what happened. You know, how I broke my leg."

Maya nodded but remained silent. Often, the longer she waited, the more a child would say.

Kiernan fidgeted, then spoke quickly. "I'm serious. I don't remember. That whole day is just…blank. The doctor says it's because I hit my head."

"That's possible," Maya said, thinking it was equally possible that the boy's brain had blocked the memory because it was too painful, because the betrayal was too great when one family member hurt another.

But even as she thought that, she felt a quiver of connection. What he had described suddenly seemed all too familiar. She took a step nearer the boy. "You've lost the entire day?"

"Most of it, anyway." His mouth twisted.

"I'm not lying, honest. I don't remember what happened. But whatever it was, it couldn't have been my dad. I know what you think, but it wasn't him. He doesn't hit. He and my mom don't believe in it." Kiernan blew out a breath. "They lecture, sure. They've grounded me once or twice, and they've taken away my Internet and my cell phone. But they don't hit."

His voice rang with sincerity, but Maya's brain had jammed on the similarity between his description and her own experience. "If you can't remember anything, you don't know for sure."

His expression clouded. "My dad doesn't hit. You have to believe me. You have to—"

"Kiernan?" a woman's voice called from the lobby. The tone scaled up an octave and cracked with stress. "Kiernan? Where are you?" Ilona Henkes's voice dropped, as though she was speaking aside to another adult, maybe one of the cops in the lobby. "He's not even supposed to be here because he can't skate yet. I told him to stay home. And now this!" Ilona raised her voice again and practically screamed, *"Kiernan!"*

The boy's face twisted with indecision

before he called, "I'm over here, Ma!" Then he turned to Maya, expression etched with urgency. "Hide. She'll be pissed if she sees me talking to you."

Maya nodded and quickly moved off, deeper into the darkened hallway, more because she wanted an opportunity to overhear the reunion than because she wanted to spare Kiernan his mother's wrath. Her mind spun with what he'd told her. The information was nothing new, but she couldn't ignore the parallels between his ex- perience and hers.

A bump on the head. Lost time.

What the hell had happened that day?

"There you are! I was so worried about you!" Ilona's voice broke on tears. "What are you doing here? I told you to stay home!" Without waiting for her son's response, she barreled on, "Are you okay? Were you near the explosion? You weren't hurt, were you?"

The voices moved away, but Maya heard the boy answer that he was fine, heard renewed ad- monishments from Ilona, who sounded exactly like the worried, well-balanced mother she had appeared throughout the investigation.

Kiernan seemed convinced his father

hadn't hurt him. Ilona had been staunch in her husband's defense. Wexton, though too smug, hadn't shaken under interrogation.

For the first time in weeks, Maya allowed herself to wonder whether she'd been wrong about Henkes.

But no, she thought, glancing around the deserted hallway and through the door to the hastily evacuated skate shop, that didn't make any sense, either. Who but Henkes would be likely to target his properties? A competitor? An enemy?

But why? What possible motive could there be?

She didn't know, and she wasn't going to figure it out standing in the hallway by herself. Now that Kiernan and his mother were gone, the coast was clear for her to return to the lobby, and from there to head to the bomb site.

And Thorne. She swallowed an unprofessional heart-thump at the thought of his name. At the thought of what they'd done. The heat of a faint blush washed across her face. She pressed both palms to her face and fought to calm her suddenly racing heart.

"Deal with it," she told herself sternly, the words echoing in the dim emptiness. "This isn't about you and Thorne. It's about catching this bastard before he kills again."

She expected an echo as her answer.

She got a masculine chuckle and a stealthy footstep.

"Who's there?" Heart pounding into her throat, she spun toward the sound, tripped and went down hard, sprawling on the polished floor.

A heavy weight landed atop her, pressing her flat, holding her still. An arm wrapped itself around her face and a hand grappled for her mouth. Something tightened around her ankle, digging into the flesh bared beneath her dress.

Panicked, she jabbed back with her elbows, twisted away and screamed, "Help! Help me! He's here! He's—"

"Quiet!" a voice hissed. She heard something rip, and a strip of sticky tape was slapped across her mouth. The pressure mashed her lips against her teeth and she screamed as best she through her nose.

The noise seemed pitiful in comparison to the rising din she could hear from the lobby.

Something else had happened. They weren't paying any attention to her.

Nobody was looking for her.

Desperation exploded in Maya's chest, in her mind, and she thrashed against the heavy weight that pinned her to the floor. She squirmed, flailed, fought to get free.

Then she *was* free. The weight disappeared. She scrambled upright, turned to run—

And her right foot was yanked out from underneath her, sending her crashing to the floor. "I don't think so," growled the shadow of a man standing over her.

Head spinning, Maya fought to focus on him, fought to identify her attacker. But a wide hand blotted out the dim light, and another piece of tape was slapped over her eyes, hard enough to make her eardrums ring.

Bastard! She screamed in the sudden darkness, but her fury came out in a pitiful mewling and her struggles made no headway against the rope he'd tied around her ankle. She made it halfway to her feet, only to be yanked back again. She crashed to the floor, choking, screaming, panicking, fighting for air, for sight, for the freedom to run back to the lobby, back to Thorne.

Her captor taped her hands together behind her back.

Thorne! She screamed his name in her mind, in her taped-shut mouth. But there was no sign of Thorne—her lover, if only for a brief interlude. No sound of pursuit, no shout of discovery, only the low hiss of her captor's labored breathing, the squeak of a shoe and the rustle of her clothing against the polished floor as he pulled on the rope and dragged her down the hallway by her ankle.

THORNE WAITED UNTIL THE coroner's assistant had bagged and transported the dead woman's body, as much for his own sake as Maya's. The corpse had looked too much like her for comfort. The women could have been sisters.

Had that been a coincidence, or another part of the plan?

When the still, black-bagged figure was wheeled out, Thorne returned to the lobby. He didn't see Maya in the open space, but what he did see gave him pause.

Ilona and Kiernan Henkes.

A surge of instinct sent him toward the pair, but Ilona saw him coming and hustled her son through the doors. Thorne took a single step after them—

And an image buffeted him. Consumed him.

Darkness. Suffocation. Fear.

"Maya!" He couldn't have said how he knew, but he did.

She was in terrible danger.

ONE MINUTE, MAYA WAS BEING dragged along the polished marble as she fought her bonds, and the next thing she knew, the floor disappeared out from beneath her. She fell and rolled down a flight of stairs, feeling their hard, cruel edges dig into her flesh with bruising force. She cried out in pain, the sound muffled by tape and fear.

Then her fall ended and she felt a flat, cold floor beneath her. She curled into a ball and whimpered with the pain, with the shock and helplessness.

"Shut up. We're almost there." He didn't whisper now, and his voice wasn't hidden behind the mechanical changer, bringing new terror.

He didn't care if she heard his voice.

He was going to kill her.

"Stay here." He lifted her by her bonds, carried her a few feet further and dumped her on the floor without warning. Her head smacked onto the unyielding floor, startling a muffled cry out of her. She grayed out for a moment, partway losing consciousness in a swirl of dots and colors behind her taped-shut lids.

When she came to, she heard him moving off to her left.

Whatever he was doing, it couldn't be good.

A jolt of adrenaline gave her new strength and she twisted against her restraints, struggling and kicking. Her sundress was scant protection from the cold, damp chill of the floor. Her right leg moved only a short distance before being brought up short with a burning yank. The bastard had tied her to something.

She scissored her leg back, trying to figure out what she was tied to, where she'd been dumped. All the while, she strained to hear something, anything that would tell her where he'd brought her. What he was doing.

He'd dragged her down a flight of stairs.

So they were still in the skating rink, down one level. But where?

And would anyone find her in time?

She held Thorne's image in her mind, the way he'd looked that afternoon, dappled in sun and shade, backlit with a pollen halo, as though he was more angel than devil, though she knew he was parts of both. Thinking of the wicked sparkle in his eyes, she strained harder and finally touched something with her outstretched foot. She squirmed in that direction, worming closer to what turned out to be a wall and a series of pipes.

Which meant she was where? In a maintenance area? She sniffed, but didn't smell soot or smoke. So she was somewhere away from the earlier blast. But where? Why?

It chilled her to think that she was being held for a reason. Her captor could have knocked her out—hell, he could have killed her, if that was the plan. But he hadn't. He'd subdued her and secreted her away from the main knot of investigators.

Knowing that the Mastermind didn't do— or order done—anything without a reason, Maya pulled against her bonds. She twisted her hands, but the tape didn't give. She rubbed her face against the floor, trying to work the adhesive loose from her eyes or mouth.

A corner near her chin gave a little, pulling at her skin as it tore away.

Success! Maya craned her neck and pried at the corner using her shoulder, which was bare and cold beneath the dress. The tape stuck to the skin of her arm and pulled free, halfway across her mouth and then all the way, letting in a blessed gulp of air.

She followed the deep breath with a loud scream. "Help! Help me, I'm down here! Thorne! Chief! Anyone, *I'm down here!*"

"Don't bother. They won't hear."

Maya froze at the sound of his voice, but forced her fears at bay. She was a professional. She could handle this. If he was talking to her, there was hope.

Or so she told herself.

"Tell me what you want," she said evenly. "I can help you. I can—"

"I've already got everything I need." She felt him move nearer, though he remained several steps away when he said, "Henkes sends his regards." The name was a splash of cold against the colder floor, the final confirmation of what she'd suspected, what nobody else had believed. But then the voice continued, "Too bad you won't get a chance to share that tidbit with any of your cop friends."

The words were followed by a splash of liquid. The sharp smell of gasoline.

And the hiss of a match being struck.

Chapter Twelve

Thorne tried the front of the building first, on the off chance that Maya had stepped outside to avoid a run-in with Ilona Henkes. When there was no sign of her near the rescue vehicles, and the cops outside swore they hadn't seen her, he ducked back into the rink with urgency humming in his veins.

Where the hell was she?

He muttered, "Damn fool woman," in an effort to convince himself that she'd wandered off on the heels of a thought. But deep down inside, he knew it was more than that.

She was in danger.

He strode down to the rink area, where the melting ice was studded with pieces of the demolished cement wall and red slicks of frozen blood.

Thorne gestured Tucker McDermott aside.

"What's wrong?" the detective asked quickly.

"I can't find Maya." The four simple words poured ice through Thorne's veins, along with the certainty that this wasn't the way it was supposed to happen. Wasn't the way it was supposed to end. "I told her to wait for me in the lobby, and now she's gone."

He'd promised to look out for her, even before they'd become lovers. Then, it had been a responsibility, a chore handed him by the chief. Now, it was a necessity.

If anything had happened to her…

"I'll get Cassie and Alissa and meet you in the lobby," McDermott said quickly.

Too jumpy to wait for the others, Thorne turned for the door and nearly slammed into Chief Parry. He stumbled back. "Sorry, Chief. I was—" He gestured vaguely.

"Thinking." The chief nodded. "That's why I brought you onto this case, Coleridge. I need your impressions, your opinions." He gestured toward the blood-spattered ice. "What do you think—"

"I can't talk right now, Chief," Thorne interrupted. "Maya's gone missing and I need all hands on deck to find her."

He turned and strode off, not waiting for the chief's okay in his haste to find Maya, to make sure she was okay. Because if she was, he was going to kill her himself for leaving the lobby.

Grinding his teeth, Thorne strode down a darkened hallway. He stuck his head into the skate shop and saw nothing out of place beyond the signs of a hasty evacuation in the wake of the explosion. The building remained secure, and would stay closed until the Forensics Department and Sawyer's bomb squad had lifted all the evidence they could find.

Anxiety thrumming in his veins, he called Maya's name, and heard it echo back unanswered.

Maya... Maya... Maya...

He returned to the hallway in time to meet the chief, McDermott and a dozen other cops approaching with grim, determined expressions on their faces.

"We'll spread out." Parry gestured half of his people in either direction, toward the hallways that encircled the main rink. "Work in pairs, two per level, one set in each direction." He glanced at Thorne. "Coleridge, you're with me. Where are we going?"

Thorne was aware of the other officers pausing a moment to listen, aware that the chief expected something he couldn't give.

Or could he?

For the first time in years, maybe ever, he consciously sought the injured part of his brain, the place Mason Falk's drugs had burned into something more than it should have been, something less. He drove his thoughts into the part of his brain he'd avoided for so long, filling it and stretching it, asking for answers.

All he got was a hollow echo of death. Of danger.

He had nothing. No flash. No instinct. Nothing except the fear that beat in his heart, the premonition that he would be too late to save her.

Too late to save himself.

"We'll go up," he said, making a decision born of pure guesswork.

The chief nodded. "Up it is." He waved the others off. "Keep in contact via radio. I've got vehicles fanning out from here in case she's left the building, but until we know what we're looking for…" He trailed off, but the inference was clear.

Without more information, there was little hope that they could find Maya if she was stashed in a car trunk, headed for God only knew where.

The image was terrifying, but it refused to fully form in Thorne's brain. It didn't seem right. Didn't jibe with the flashes he'd been fighting for too long now, ever since he'd pushed his sunglasses low and gotten his first good look into her eyes.

Cursing, he strode to the far door and pushed through into the utilitarian stairwell, which was done in gray concrete and heavy metal railings.

"Did you hear that?" the chief said suddenly. He leaned over the railing and peered down. "I thought I heard—"

He broke off just as Thorne heard it, too.

A woman's voice calling for help.

Nearly drowned out by the crackle of flames.

THE HEAT WAS ALMOST MORE terrifying for the darkness. Maya's mind and body told her she should be seeing the flames, should be watching them march toward her in those last few final moments. But she couldn't see a damn thing because her eyes were taped shut.

She could only listen to the crackle and hiss of the fire, feel the searing heat on her skin and smell the gasoline her captor had poured on her clothes.

She wasn't on fire yet, but cold, deadly logic told her it was only a matter of time. He must have lit a pool of accelerant some distance away from the splash line around her body. Maybe he'd wanted her scared before she died, or maybe he hadn't wanted to watch the actual immolation.

He'd left her alone to wait.

And scream.

She tried it again, though her throat already ached from dozens of unanswered cries. "Help me! Help! I'm down here!" Her voice broke on the last two words, cracked on sobs that felt dry because her tears were trapped beneath a wide swath of sticky tape. She was dizzy, disoriented, desperate.

"Damn it, somebody help me!" She yanked at her tied ankle and felt the rope cut deeper into her flesh. She twisted at the tape on her wrists, but it didn't yield, didn't give.

She heard a sputter and crackle. The sound

of flames moving nearer. Any moment now, they would jump from one pool of gasoline to the next and she would become a human torch.

Burned alive. Burned to death.

Panic rose, final and absolute, swamping her, suffocating her. In the final moments of her life, as the heat singed her skin and the flames roared higher, closer, she wished she'd done things differently, wished she'd been more open with her feelings and her history, been more demanding when it came to the things she wanted. The things she needed.

Damn it, she wished she'd done more, *been* more.

The voice of the fire increased until it sounded like words. Like a voice. Thorne's voice, shouting, "Here! She's in here!"

At first Maya thought she was imagining it, that her mind had conjured his memory to keep her company in her final moments.

Then she heard the deep-throated roar of a fire extinguisher, and felt the splatter of cooling foam, the grasp of strong hands on her bare arms, lifting her, dragging her as she had been dragged before.

"Hey! Let go!" She thrashed, struggling to

free herself, not sure whether the hands belonged to rescue or new danger.

"Hold on," Thorne's voice said. "This is going to hurt."

She forced herself to relax only moments before he ripped the tape away from her eyes. She screamed reflexively, though the gasoline had softened the adhesive, dulling the pain.

"Sorry." His voice was ragged sounding over the continued puffs of the extinguisher. "God, are you okay?"

"I'm not sure." Maya waited while her vision cleared from dark to painful white, solidifying into the image of Thorne's face, creased in concerned lines. His hands gripped her arms hard enough to bruise, but she wished they were even tighter, because the ache proved she was alive. "He said it was Henkes," she gasped. "He said the name, said the fire was a message from Henkes." She glanced beyond him and felt her stomach dip. "Oh, God."

They were in a maintenance area, as she had surmised. Black streaks marked the walls and floor, and the whole place stank of gasoline. She could see where the bastard had poured a pool of the accelerant, then a thin trickle leading toward her.

"Why didn't it light all the way?" she asked, her words cracking on the horror of the question, or maybe from the force of her screams.

"I don't know." Thorne's voice sounded as ragged as hers, and he didn't let go of her arms. His eyes searched hers as though looking for something and not finding it. "He set a trail to delay the fire by a few minutes. Something must've gone wrong."

Or it went right, she thought, because that mistake had saved her life as surely as the men who now crowded the room, filling it with fire retardant foam and starting blowers to clear the fumes. Aloud, she said, "I'm fine. You can let go of me now."

Thorne looked at his hands on her arms, and the indentations his fingers had made on her flesh, but he didn't step away. "Not on your life." He kept his grip on one arm, turned, and half dragged, half led her out of the room. "Come on."

Maya nearly tripped over her own feet when her rubbery legs failed to keep up with his long strides. "Where are we going?"

"To get you cleaned up before somebody lights a cigarette near you," he grated, not slackening pace even as they passed a knot of cops in the hall that included the chief, Tucker McDermott and Alissa. Maya saw Alissa's eyes darken with worry, saw her mouth stretch to say something, but Thorne blew past the group before the friends could connect.

Maya thought about digging in her heels, but he was right, damn him. She stank of gasoline and was a hazard to herself and others. Getting clean would have to come first, explanations second.

As if she could explain what had happened to her.

Thorne let go of her abruptly, ducked into the skate shop, grabbed a warm-up suit off one of the racks and tossed two twenties on the deserted counter. He handed the suit to her and nodded toward the nearby restroom. "Change and leave your clothes for Alissa and Cassie. They might get some contact evidence." He leaned against the wall and crossed his arms over his chest. "If you're not out in three minutes, I'm coming in."

Maya didn't argue. She didn't have the

strength, or maybe she had too much strength, all of it pulsing just beneath her skin in wave after wave of tremors. She wanted to shake, wanted to howl, wanted to burst into tears or scream until her voice gave out for good. She wanted to grab Thorne tightly, or shove him away with both hands and run.

She wanted too many things all at once. Because of it, she nodded without a word and pushed past him into the bathroom.

She was changed in under three minutes, and gladly left her gas-soaked dress, panties, bra, socks and shoes on the bathroom floor. The warm-up suit was cheap nylon, and chafed across her damp skin. Shivers traveled from her skin inwards, until her whole body shook with them.

She had very nearly died.

If Thorne hadn't come for her…

She shivered, pulled the nylon zip-up suit close around her scalded-feeling skin, and pushed through the swinging door, out into the hallway, which was now lit day-bright.

She squinted. "Guess they've got the power back up."

He didn't answer, just stared at her with

those blank, buffered eyes until she had to fight not to squirm under his regard. Anger crackled around him like a visible aura, but he didn't make a move toward her, didn't yell as she knew he wanted to. Instead, he inclined his head and gestured toward the front of the building. "Come on. Let's go."

Fatigue and tension pulled at her, and her too-sensitive skin told her she was freezing cold, though the hallway was warm around them. She nodded. "Right. The chief will want his report."

But once they'd bypassed the last of the rescue workers outside the rink and pushed through the first of the avid, news-hungry reporters, once they were in his car and headed away, Thorne turned them deeper into the city without a word, bypassing the PD. When he pulled into the parking garage beneath her building, Maya nearly wept with relief.

She waited for him to get her door because she was too numb, too unsettled to do otherwise. They rode up in the elevator, shoulder to shoulder, silence stretching between them like a bad smell. He was furious. She was shaky.

Bad combination, she knew. She needed

her armor in place, her shields raised before she could go up against him. In her current state, she was likely to agree to just about anything.

And hate him for it later.

It wasn't until she reached her door that she realized her purse was gone. She shaped her hands in front of her, as though the bag might magically appear slung over her shoulder. "I lost my... It must've flung free when he grabbed me. I don't..." Tears pressed against her eyelids, weak and useless. "I don't have a key."

All she wanted to do was go home, but she was barred from even that.

"Make sure nobody's watching," Thorne ordered. "I'll take care of it."

"How?" She glanced quickly up and down, but the hallway outside her condo was deserted. When she saw the slim metal lock picks in his hands, she hissed, "Where did you get those?"

"It's a habit I picked up undercover." He popped the lock in under a minute, and returned the tools to the inner pocket of his jacket. "They say it never hurts to have a second skill."

But although his words bordered on light, his expression remained closed as he ushered her through into the condo, then made her wait by the door while he checked the rooms. Though the building was under constant surveillance, the Mastermind had proven himself able to get past the cops before.

"All clear?" she said when he rejoined her, expression dark.

"There's nobody here but us," he said, which seemed like more of a threat than an answer. Sure enough, he continued, "Which means I can ask you what the hell you thought you were doing. I told you to wait in the lobby. You were safe there. What the hell happened?"

His volume climbed with each word and he loomed closer and closer, until his angry eyes nearly dominated her vision and his breath was a hot, spicy wash on her face.

Maya had thought she would bow under the pressure, maybe even break. Instead, she felt the anger build. The desire to give in was washed away by a surge of frustration, a kick of rage against the people and events that had conspired against her ever since her arrival in Bear Claw. She'd come to town looking to build her career, to protect the innocent citizens of the Colorado town.

Instead, she had become a target.

Well, no more. She was done being a target, done being a victim. She balled her fists at her sides and held her voice steady so it wouldn't crack weakly when she said, "That's enough." When he drew back, surprised, she followed and poked a finger toward his chest. "I've had it up to the teeth with you bossing me around, making decisions for me, making calls about the case without consulting me…" She trailed off, sorting through the resentments until she found the central issue. "I'm done being treated like a second-class cop. Maybe I made a mistake with Henkes, maybe not. But mistakes happen—we fix them and move on. You want a partner? Fine. Treat me like a partner. You want a lover? Then you'd better damn well start treating me like one of those, too. But I'm sick and tired of you treating me like you're some police force big brother. Yes, you've got seniority, and yes, you've had field experiences that I can't begin to understand, but that does *not*," she emphasized the word with another finger stab toward his chest, "entitle you to treat me like your dim-witted little sister."

"I didn't—"

"I don't care," she interrupted, not wanting to hear his explanation or defense. "In fact, I don't care about much of anything right now. I smell of gasoline, my bruises have bruises and my skin feels like I'm sunburned all over. I want a cool shower and a colder drink—a soda, damn it—and then I want us to sit down and talk about this like professionals. If you can't do that, then I want you gone when I get out of the shower. You either accept me as an equal, or we're not working together. I don't give a damn anymore that I'm suspended. I'm not even sure I give a damn if you take my job when this is all over. But I am *not*," this time she emphasized the word by turning away and heading for the bathroom, tossing her parting shot over her shoulder, "*absolutely* not allowing that bastard to go free."

It was Henkes, damn it. Her attacker had said it plain as day.

She entered the small bathroom and closed the door behind her, oddly surprised that Thorne hadn't followed, that he hadn't argued harder. Worse, moments later she heard the sound of the front door locking shut.

Disappointment and a spiky sense of betrayal washed through her.

He'd left, damn him.

Granted she'd told him to, but she'd never expected him to listen. Fuming and inexplicably heartsore, she shucked off the cheap nylon suit and cranked on the shower. Her hair felt greasy, her body felt grimy and her skin throbbed with the blood flowing just beneath it. Cool water would feel good, she told herself, and ignored the vague beat of depression at the knowledge that Thorne was gone.

She'd thought their moment together in the garden had meant something, that the worry in his eyes when he'd saved her had been personal, despite their differences.

Apparently, she'd been wrong.

Ignoring the faint sting of tears, she climbed into the shower and let out a broken sigh when the cool spray sluiced over her skin and the hiss of the drumming water drowned out the real world, at least for a few minutes.

"I don't think of you as a sister, but I can't think of you as a cop."

Maya screamed at the sound of his voice and yanked the curtain aside so she could see out but he couldn't see in. "What the hell are you doing in here?"

Thorne stood in her bathroom, fully clothed and smelling faintly of gasoline. There was a small bruise under his left eye, one she hadn't noticed earlier. She noticed it now because his expression was different, more open. Almost baffled.

"Damn it, you're not just a cop to me, Maya." He let out a long breath and held his hands away from his sides as though indicating that he was unarmed. "You're a woman. My woman."

The last two words seemed ripped from his chest, from his gut, and they punched through her like power.

Still, she stared at him for a long beat, not willing to accept. "What are you saying?"

He sighed again, and the last of the barriers fell from his eyes, leaving them clear and hazel, and looking just as confused and stirred-up as she was. "I'm saying that I'm falling for you and I don't know what the hell to do about it."

Maya let that lie for a moment while

warmth unfurled in her chest and beat beneath her fire-sensitized skin, counteracting the cool of the shower. She waited while the truth of it suffused her, chasing away the fears.

Then she snaked a bare arm out of the shower and wrapped her fingers in the front of his wrinkled shirt, thinking that the outside world would have to take care of itself for an hour. "I know what we can do about it."

And she pulled him into the shower, fully dressed.

Chapter Thirteen

Thorne didn't trust the leap of joy when the lukewarm water hit his face, followed quickly by her lips. He didn't believe the click of rightness when she curled her arms around his neck and pressed herself—all that wet, slick nakedness—against his fully clothed, rapidly heating body. But he couldn't escape the want, the lust that roared through his veins and left him dizzy, left him reeling.

I'm falling for you. He hadn't meant to say that, hadn't meant to put himself out there like that, especially not under these circumstances. But once the words were out there, they'd sounded so damn right.

He didn't love her, but he wanted her. Needed her.

Maybe that would be enough for now.

"I'll make it be enough," he said, and when she pulled back to look at him askance, he amended it to, "It'll never be enough. Kiss me again."

She did, kissing him, twining around him until he wouldn't have been sure where she left off and he began if it weren't for the wet bind of his clothes. He struggled with his shirt while he kissed her, while the water pounded down on him, feeling cold against the heat that flared through his body, pounded in his blood.

Then his shirt was free and her hands were on him, their torsos pressed skin to skin for the first time, creating new, maddening friction. Her breasts pressed into him, soft and pliable. He eased back to slide his hands up and capture the small globes. Her nipples pebbled at his touch and the round weight of her settled in his palms, small and perfect.

Simply perfect.

"Here, let me," she whispered, and he felt her fingers on his belt, on the button and zipper of his pants, and he could do little more than close his eyes and savor the sensation, the anticipation. He felt his entire being expand and harden. His heart expanded, his senses expanded until it seemed that he could sense every molecule in the room, that he could taste the air as she did, feel the pound of water as she did.

He felt the final mental barrier fall away and he didn't give a damn. He opened himself to the heightened sensations, to the feeling of finally being in the right place and time with the right woman. He laid himself bare to the tug of her fingers, to the wet slickness of her skin beneath his touch, and the heat of her mouth against his.

When she pulled away, she was breathless and laughing. She tugged at the soaked material of his pants and boxers, which had bound at his hips, tangled and immovable. "You'll have to do it. I'm stumped."

"You got it." He stepped away to strip off the remainder of his clothes in a quick, effective move that lacked elegance but got the job done. Then, instead of moving back toward her, he stood and spread his hands.

He had intended to give her one last chance to run, though he knew damn well it was too late for either of them to escape. But his breath caught on the words and his hands fell to his sides when he looked at her, really *looked* at her in all her naked glory.

"Perfect," he breathed, the single word startled out of him by the sight of her, by the fist of emotion that punched him just beneath the heart.

They had come together outside in the garden space, mostly clothed, but not caring as the need had burned between them. He'd come away with the memory of soft skin and wet, hot kisses, and the thundering power of the connection when they had joined on the physical level.

Now it was different. Now it was more. *She* was more. She was everything.

He'd known she was small, but her big personality had pushed that knowledge to the back of his mind. And oddly, he'd fallen for—yes, he liked that term—he'd fallen for her brain, for her single-minded if sometimes potentially misdirected determination to prove herself and bring the Mastermind to justice. He'd grown used to her quiet resolve, and found himself looking forward to her sly flashes of humor, her open flashes of anger.

So yes, he'd fallen for her mind, her soul. But now he was reminded that she had one hell of a body, too. Her pink-tipped breasts were small and perfectly formed, and her finely muscled shoulders balanced the shallow curve of her hips, defining a waist that he could nearly span with his hands. Her legs weren't long but they curved perfectly, and they joined at a narrow line of dark hair that appeared sculpted by some feminine wile into a curving T that beckoned him. Invited him.

"You're perfect," he said, not realizing he'd spoken aloud until the words carried over the hiss of the shower, breaking the silence between them.

Her lips curved. "No, I'm not. But thank you." Before he could respond to that, or put words to the images cramming his brain, she tilted her head and gave him a long look, up and down and back, bringing his blood to a boil. Her lips curved. "For what it's worth, I'm crazy about you."

He stiffened momentarily, then smiled when the panic didn't come. *Crazy about you* he could deal with. It wasn't *I love you.*

It didn't ever have to be.

"Ditto," he said. He wrapped his hands around her waist and boosted her up, so their mouths were aligned. They met halfway in a kiss, then another and another yet again, soft touches that soothed and heated at the same time, then stronger, longer, deeper, searching kisses that rocked Thorne to his very core as she lifted her legs and wrapped them around his hips.

The water dwindled to a warmer trickle, though he wasn't sure if they'd run the boiler out or if she'd turned the shower down. The warm dribble flowed over them, between them, slicking and warming and adding a new level of pleasure.

Of need.

Her fingers dug into his shoulders, then slid down to fasten on to his biceps as she gave herself up to his support, to a position that aligned them perfectly. She cradled his hard, throbbing manhood at the juncture of her thighs, along that neatly trimmed T of dark hair and darker, hotter promises.

His body howled for entrance, for completion, for a joining that was fuller, faster, harder than their quick, furtive coupling in the garden. But he held himself back, refusing to rush this time, determined to make sure she was ready, even if it meant going painfully past ready himself.

He turned and pressed her against the cool tile wall, using the corner to support her, to support himself as he kissed her jaw, her neck, the hollow behind her ear. She moaned and he wallowed in the heat and the glory of it as he returned to her lips. Her mouth drew him in and her tongue trapped him, held him in her thrall as she unlinked one foot from behind him, used it to brace herself on the door molding, and shifted up against him, then down again, seating his hardness within her.

Thorne was unprepared for the move, for the heat and the slick wetness that suddenly held him, caressed him, closed around him until there was nothing, only that hot, wet clamp that commanded his entire attention.

He was dimly aware that something wasn't right, but the perfection of their joining swept away the doubts and concerns, expanding his consciousness away from himself and into her, into the room at large until he swore he could taste the difference between each of their kisses as the water trickled between them, adding the sharp tang of iron to her womanly bouquet. He heard the drum of the water, the thump of faraway pipes, and the cry of a bird outside or maybe a child in a nearby unit. He was aware of everything, connected to everything in a way he hadn't been since he'd come down off Mason Falk's mountain.

He sucked in a shuddering breath, pressed his cheek to hers, began to move inside her—

And the world contracted to a single point of contact, to the two of them and nothing else as he withdrew from her and thrust back in on a surge of heat and sensation. He groaned, or maybe she did, he wasn't sure anymore where he left off and she began, he only knew that this was right, this was perfect, this was what they'd been heading toward since the moment they'd met, years earlier.

"Again," she breathed, and he complied, withdrawing from her and thrusting forward in a smooth slide that set off chain reaction detonations deep in his belly, and higher up, in his chest, where a fist tightened around his heart, squeezing until he could barely draw breath.

But who needed to breathe when he had Maya?

Scattered droplets of warm water flicked across his shoulders, streaming between them in sparkling rivulets. He bent and touched his mouth to the wetness at her shoulder, drinking her, reveling in her.

His body moved again, finding a rhythm far older than him, one that rose and heated and blotted out everything but the feel of her against him, around him, the feel of her fingernails digging into his arms and the sound of her voice at his temple, whispering his name, urging him on, chanting for him to move faster, harder, the words echoing in tandem with the beat of his blood and the slap of shower-slicked flesh coming together in a frenzy of need and want.

Harder. Faster.

He held her tighter, wanting to know she was with him. She bit his shoulder and he growled deep in his throat, unprepared for the jolt of heat, of power. She met him stroke for stroke, taking more, demanding more until he was buried to the hilt with each thrust, only on his feet because his legs were locked and the walls were solid at her back. His breath rattled in his lungs, oxygen seeming not nearly as important as the woman in his arms.

Suddenly, though not suddenly at all, she

bowed back, arching her breasts into him and vising her legs around his hips. *"Thorne!"*

Her inner muscles clamped around him, pulling him into her, holding him at that deepest, fullest point. She shuddered against him and raked her nails down his water-slicked arms, across his back and ribs, trembling with the force of her climax. Her excitement fueled his and he pressed into her, against her, holding her tightly.

Mine, he thought as he came. *Mine.*

But even as some insane part of him spoke of deeper, frightening feelings, another surge rose up and caught him, swamped him with the weight of its power.

The flash came out of nowhere, giving him no time to shield himself, no time to prepare for the vision.

This time he saw all of it, saw what he had done in the past.

What he would do in the near future.

BEFORE THE AFTERSHOCKS COULD fade, before the glow could form, Maya felt Thorne jerk away from her. He staggered back, eyes wild, leaving her to stand braced against the shower wall, naked and wet.

Her belly clutched. "Thorne? What's wrong?"

"Nothing," he croaked, but it was clearly a lie.

Something was very wrong.

Maya's sex-tingled body chilled at the panic in Thorne's eyes. Suddenly feeling very naked, she lifted one hand to her belly, the other to her breasts. "Thorne? Talk to me." When he didn't respond, she touched his arm and shivered at the cool wetness of his flesh, as the sultry moisture of the shower morphed to a dank chill. "Come on. Let's get dried off and dressed, and you can tell me what just happened. One minute, we were—" She shook her head. "Never mind. We can deal with it."

But when she exited the shower, grabbed a pair of fluffy towels and turned back to offer him one, she found he hadn't moved. He was still staring at her, face frightening in its blankness.

"I shouldn't have done that." He ignored the towel and bent to grab his sodden clothing. He wrung his shirt out and yanked it over his shoulders, then did the same with his pants, pulling them on with vicious strength. He jammed his feet into his wet shoes and grated, "I know better, damn it."

He brushed past her and stalked out into the hallway. It wasn't until Maya heard the rattle of the deadbolt that she realized he was walking out on her.

Temper flaring, she yanked the towel around her and folded it over, so it would more or less stay in place when she ran across the condo and slapped a hand on the door as he opened it. "Don't you dare! You'd better talk to me, or else—"

"Or else what?" He opened the door, forcing her back and emphasizing the fact that he out-weighed her by a good sixty pounds, and out-muscled her by more than that. He started to say something more, then stopped and hissed out a breath. His voice dropped low when he said, "I'm sorry, I know this looks bad."

"I don't know *what* it looks like." Realizing that her tone bordered on hysterical, she took a breath and lowered her voice. "I deserve better than this and you know it. If you're walking out, you at least owe me an explanation." Nerves fluttered in her chest as she waited for him to deny it, to tell her he wasn't walking out.

Instead, he turned back and eased the door partway shut. "I can't do this. I thought I could, but I can't. I've just gotten out of a relationship with another cop and I promised myself I wouldn't go there again. It's too messy." But there was something else in his eyes, something darker and more dangerous.

"I don't believe you." She closed her fingers on his arm, feeling the damp material of his shirt. "Try again." She thought back to the last moments of their lovemaking, to the shock of bare skin.

Bare skin!

"We didn't use a condom," she said, and felt him flinch beneath her touch. "Is that what has you spooked? It's okay, assuming you don't have any dreaded diseases. I'm on the pill."

There was barely a flicker of reaction in his eyes. "That's good to know."

She got it then. "We were skin to skin and it triggered a vision. What did you see?" She tightened her fingers on his forearm, feeling them dig into flesh. *"Tell me!"*

He looked down at her for a long moment, pupils so wide his eyes looked nearly black. Finally, he grated, "I saw you die." He took a long shuddering breath. "I heard the gunshot. I heard you scream and I smelled your blood."

Maya's fingers slipped from his arm and she stumbled back, shock buzzing through her system. A wide, yawning pit opened up in her stomach and she pressed the back of one hand to her mouth to hold in the cry, the nausea.

"I swear to God I won't let it happen," Thorne said, voice rough with emotion. "I'll do whatever it takes."

"Who—" She swallowed hard to clear the hard lump from her throat. "Who kills me?"

He looked at her long and hard. "I do."

And then he slipped through the door and slammed it gunshot-loud.

A sob tore itself from Maya's throat as the stress and fear of the past few days closed in on her. She flung herself at the door and shot the deadbolt, then activated the new security system, as though that would keep the fear at bay.

I do. Thorne's words echoed in her skull, vibrating with the rage she'd seen from him, the banked violence she'd sensed within him.

Yet still she didn't believe, didn't understand. Thorne wasn't a killer.

"There has to be another explanation," she said aloud, and heard the words bounce back at her from the too-close walls. She headed for the bedroom, needing to get dressed and figure out what had just happened, what was going to come next.

She found herself in the kitchen, instead, with the rum bottle in one hand, a glass in the other.

"Damn it!" Anger built. Anger at her teenage self for making stupid choices that had taken a life. Anger at Dane for spending two years in a minimum-security facility for vehicular manslaughter and emerging just as cocky, just as hard-partying as he'd gone in. Anger at her grown-up self for still being weak.

She couldn't resist Thorne.

She couldn't resist the pull of the rum.

"No, damn it. That's not me. Not anymore. I don't need to drink to be strong." She clenched her teeth and uncapped the bottle. Held it just shy of her lips and inhaled, smelling the sharp tang of oblivion.

Then she upended the bottle in the sink.

THORNE HELD HIS EMOTIONS in check as he drove to his motel room, changed into dry clothes and packed everything he'd brought with him.

He knew he'd hurt Maya, and knew it would be worse when she learned that he'd left without saying goodbye. But what was the alternative? She wouldn't be safe until he left town.

She won't be safe then, either, his instincts told him. *The Mastermind is still out there. He's still after her.*

True, but if she left town, she would have only one murderer after her.

If he stayed, she'd have two.

In the weeks and months following Thorne's escape from Mason Falk's compound, he'd talked to dozens of people ranging from his superiors to a bevy of counselors savvy in posttraumatic stress. Their message was clear. If he hadn't killed Falk's lieutenant, Donny Greek, he wouldn't have escaped. In captivity, he wouldn't have survived long enough to see the Wagon Ridge PD storm the mountain, take the militiamen into custody and bring down Falk's cult once and for all.

It had been self-defense. Justifiable homicide. He could accept that intellectually, if not emotionally.

What he couldn't accept, what he couldn't discuss with the others, with anyone else in the six years since the incident was the fact that he'd enjoyed the killing.

Even now, he sometimes awoke remembering the feel of Greek's throat in his hands, the other man's pulse fluttering beneath his thumbs, slower and slower as life ebbed. Even now, Thorne could picture how the gloating in the bastard's eyes had changed to fear, then outright panic as the darkness closed in.

Even now, he remembered the hot rush of triumph, of power.

Of satisfaction.

Killing doesn't make you a killer, they had told him.

Maybe not, but enjoying it did.

"I hated Greek," Thorne grated, aware that the motel room was dim and dark around him as the day faded to night. He'd hated how Donny Greek had taken the women of the encampment, sometimes even other men's wives, and how the men hadn't argued, how they'd been too afraid to protest.

He'd hated the women's screams, and how he hadn't been able to help them when he was undercover, how he'd been even less able to help once he was captured.

"I don't hate Maya," Thorne said aloud. He tipped his head back and stared at the ceiling while her words replayed in his mind. *I'm crazy about you,* she'd said.

Hell, he was crazy about her, too. So how was it that he could picture her death, imagine the feel of the trigger beneath his fingers, the kick of recoil in his hands?

He could smell her blood and see the look in her eyes, the surprise that crossed her face just before she dropped to an expensive-looking Oriental carpet. And in his heart of hearts, the horror was mingled with satisfaction.

The feeling of a job well done.

"Which is why I'm going to stay the hell away from her," he said, climbing to his feet and heading for the door. "I'm going to get out of here before I can do anything to her."

But, as he headed to the car, and from there to the Bear Claw PD, a truth echoed within his skull.

He had yet to outrun one of his premonitions.

They all came true in the end.

BY THE TIME MAYA'S HAIR WAS dry, she had decided two things. One, she wasn't staying under house arrest. She was a cop, suspended or not. She knew how to handle herself without Thorne's help and she was damn well going to manage it, starting now. And two, she wasn't letting him get away with whatever he'd just pulled. She was going to confront him and make him talk to her.

"I don't buy that vision crap," she said aloud, forcing strength into her voice. "If he doesn't want to be with me, he should say so."

Knowing she was going into battle, she dressed carefully. Her bruises were still sore, and her skin was tender all over from the fire, and perhaps a little from the lovemaking—she refused to call it anything else, regardless of where Thorne's head was at—but she steeled herself for work clothes.

The damned sundress had gotten her into too much trouble. More importantly, she wanted the professional shield of her office attire. So she pulled on tailored black pants and a white button-down shirt, and jazzed it up with a Navajo belt and a breezy turquoise scarf.

Then she strapped on her mid-back holster

and loaded it with her spare weapon, which she'd neglected to mention when the chief had taken her service revolver. She no longer had a permit to carry concealed, but what was one more infraction added to her list?

When she was done, she checked the effect in the mirror and winced when a hollow-eyed, drawn-looking woman stared back at her. She lifted her hand to her collarbone, where the faint beginnings of a love bite blushed near the open collar of her shirt.

"Pull yourself together," she ordered. "You knew the rules going in. He doesn't do love. Neither do you."

But the final three words rang false, telling her once and for all that she did love, all right, but she'd been too late to figure that out.

More importantly, she'd picked the wrong guy. He'd said *I'm falling for you,* but what he'd really meant was *I want you, but the moment we're done I'll be out of here so fast your head'll spin.*

Anger carried her out of the condo and down to the parking garage, where she did her damnedest to banish images of Thorne's Interceptor. But the memories kept coming, frustrating her. Annoying her.

How had he become such an integral part of her existence in such a short period of time? How could such a thing happen so quickly?

"Well, it'll have to unhappen just as quickly," she said aloud, and froze when an echo of sound answered her from deeper within the parking garage.

It sounded like an indrawn breath.

Nerves prickled to life along the back of her neck, the feeling of being watched, of not being alone anymore. Instead of calling out, she jabbed her key into the door lock and cursed when it jammed.

Since when did her hands shake?

Since you became the target of a murderer, a sly stealthy voice said in her head. *Since Thorne left you unprotected and told you to stay the hell inside where you'd be safe from the killer. Safe from him.*

The latter thought brought a bigger shudder, and her hands were well and truly shaking by the time she got the door unlocked on the second try and yanked open the door. She slammed the door and fumbled to fit the key in the ignition, knowing she'd heard that sound, knowing there was someone in the garage with her.

She nearly flooded the engine trying to get the car started, and damn near sobbed with relief when it caught. She floored it and pulled of the garage going way too fast, but for a change she didn't care. She wanted to get out of there and regroup.

She was a cop, true, but she was a cop without backup.

She pulled out into traffic and headed for the Bear Claw PD, needing to talk with Thorne. They couldn't leave things they way they had. It was too awful. Too confusing.

She wouldn't beg, but nor would she let him walk away from what they had without a fight. She was too strong now for that.

When she'd nearly reached the parking lot, her cell phone rang, making her jump.

Her heart lurched up into her throat with two thoughts. What if it was Thorne, calling to apologize?

Worse, what if it wasn't?

She debated ignoring it, but that would be cowardice, so she flipped open the unit and held it to her ear. "Cooper here."

"I caught you. Good." The masculine voice sent a jolt through her system before she realized it wasn't Thorne. The tones were too guttural, almost melancholy.

"Chief Parry?"

"Affirmative. We just got a call from the Henkes residence." His voice grew, if possible, more dour. "The mother is asking to speak with you. Says the kid has something to say."

Maya's breath caught in her throat when she remembered Kiernan pulling her aside in the skating rink. Remembered being grabbed immediately after. "Is that even legal? They've got an order out against me."

"I'll testify that you were invited if it comes to that," the chief answered. "Get over there. I'll send someone to back you up."

"Not Thorne," she said too quickly, then backpedaled. "Send me someone else. Alissa or Cassie, maybe, or Tucker McDermott."

"You're not really in a position to be rearranging work orders, are you? Just get over there and see what they have."

The connection went dead, leaving Maya in the PD parking lot, staring at the phone.

What the hell?

What could Ilona or Kiernan want to tell her? Why her? Why now?

As possibilities ranging from tantalizing to ludicrous spooled through her mind, Maya glanced at the rear door of the PD. She could go in and collect her backup, make things easier.

Then she remembered the strange tone in the chief's voice, and the fact that he and Wexton Henkes were friends. She remembered the cold, dead look in Thorne's eyes when he'd left her condo and the door closed at his back.

Suddenly, the PD didn't seem like the safe zone it once had. Her fellow officers didn't seem like quite the allies she needed.

Making a quick decision, Maya spun the car in a one-eighty and headed back out onto the road, bound for the Henkes mansion. Let the chief send whatever backup he wanted. She was handling this on her own. She needed to prove this to herself, and to Thorne.

She was strong enough to do this on her own.

But because she also wasn't dumb, she flipped open her cell and hit the button for Cassie's number. When it rang through to voice mail, she said, "Cass, it's me. I'm on my way to the Henkes place and I've got a feeling..." She trailed off, unable to put a name to the nerves. "Never mind. Meet me there if you can. Grab Alissa and Tucker just in case. Leave Thorne out of it if possible, things are...let's just say things are weird between us right now." She drew breath to explain further, but a digital beep cut her off, letting her know that she'd exceeded her recording time.

It was just as well, she supposed. What else was there to say? *Thorne is convinced he's psychic, but it's really just a defense mechanism. He doesn't want me enough to work on it.*

Yeah, Cassie really didn't need that message on her machine.

But as Maya turned away from downtown Bear Claw, toward the ritzy section of town, she had a feeling that she'd left something out of her message to Cassie. Something important.

She just didn't know what it was.

HE WAITED ON THE Bear Claw Creek overpass, knowing that Drew Wilson would be late for their meeting, just because he could be. Wilson was cocky like that. He was also smart, which made him a more formidable puzzle piece than the others had been.

Wilson had executed his orders flawlessly, getting himself hired on at the prison and then biding his time, waiting until the planner was ready to take the next step. The younger man—motivated by money rather than the love of crime as the others had been—had orchestrated things perfectly at the ranch, and then again at the college skating rink. The Bear Claw cops were chasing their own stubby tails, nudged into chaos by a few well-placed distractions.

The Mastermind's lips curved in the darkness.

It was nearly time for the final, most important step, the one that would have the city hailing him as their savior.

Their hero.

He liked the ring of that.

A passing car slowed, then pulled in ahead of his vehicle and stopped. Drew Wilson climbed out and sauntered over, briefly lit by the headlights of another vehicle that crossed the bridge, headed for somewhere else.

"Hey, boss." Wilson's greeting held a faint

sneer, a reminder that he had leverage over his superior, the threat of disclosure.

Or so he thought.

"Wilson." The Mastermind nodded to his underling. "You've done well."

"You pay well," the former prison guard replied. "And speaking of which, I think it's time for us to renegotiate our deal. It seems to me that our original terms aren't as, shall we say, equitable as they could be?"

"By all means." The Mastermind reached down to the duffel at his feet. "But let's get this first business out of the way, shall we?" He lifted the heavy bag and palmed the blade he had concealed within, feeling his heart pick up a beat at the thought of what was to come.

Wilson reached for the bag. "Let's consider this a payment on account, shall we? I was thinking my new pay scale should work in arrears, starting with this last job. Getting away from the rink was tougher than it should have been. I almost didn't make it."

And you wouldn't have made it at all without my help, the Mastermind thought with an inward sneer. But outwardly, he feigned a wince. "Ouch. You've got me by the shorties. But I'm sure we can work something out. In fact—" He broke off as another set of headlights cut through the darkness, and motioned the other man closer. "Come here. I've got another job for you—at the new pay rate, of course."

Wilson's eyes lit greedily and he leaned forward just as the Mastermind lifted his blade.

The finely honed steel cut through Wilson's flesh as if it were warm butter, and grated on a rib before slipping beneath and finding its target.

The Mastermind caught his underling as he fell, and propped up the dying man. The car passed and drove on, not wanting to bother the men on the bridge.

Especially not when one of them drove a police vehicle with bubble lights atop the dome.

When the car was gone and the bridge was quiet and dark, the Mastermind cleaned and pocketed his blade, and eased the body over the railing. It landed with a splash, and the moonlight shone on the corpse as it eddied briefly in a swirl of creek water before heading downstream.

It would be found the following day, once the sun came up.

Exactly as planned.

Chapter Fourteen

Thorne was sitting at his—Maya's—desk staring at the stacked scraps of paper for the hundredth time when Cassie walked into the office. He cursed under his breath at the sight of Maya's prickly friend. He wasn't feeling up for another battle.

Hell, he wasn't even sure what he was doing at the PD. He'd been on his way out of town when the thought had struck him, sending him back to his notes. But the impulse was gone now, leaving him frustrated with the knowledge that he was close to a breakthrough, yet too far.

He glanced over at Cassie. "You need something?"

She bristled. "This is my office. I don't need a reason to be here."

"Good point." Thorne returned his attention to the file he'd pulled up on the computer, which compared the timelines of the kidnappings, the murders and the most recent attacks. Something niggled at the back of his brain, some connection that hadn't quite formed yet. He frowned and concentrated, trying to figure out which note was jarring him, which set of circumstances didn't quite jibe.

But concentrating was damn difficult when Cassie was standing across the room, arms folded, glowering at him.

He finally sighed, clicked the monitor to the screen saver and turned to face her. "Look, if there's something you want to say, say it. Otherwise, go be somewhere else. You're bothering me."

"You're going to hurt Maya, aren't you?"

Thorne jolted, then realized she was talking about emotional pain, not gunshots and blood. He shook his head. "No, I won't. I—"

He broke off, knowing that it was already too late.

Cassie's eyes darkened. "What did you do to her? Where is she?"

"She's at home," he said, answering the safer of the two questions. When she took a step closer to him, fists lifted as though she was considering slugging him one, he grimaced. "Look, what's between Maya and me isn't—"

"Don't even try it," she growled. "Maya may come off as totally settled and serene, but she's the softest one of the three of us by far. She wounds easily. She might bury the hurt deep, but it's there."

Thorne winced. "I know. I know about all of it. Her ex. The accident. All of it." When Cassie's eyes narrowed consideringly, he shook his head. "It wouldn't work between us. Trust me, I'm doing her a favor."

Cassie snorted. "No, you're not. You're doing yourself a favor. Things got too intense and you're running."

Her words resonated too deeply. He rose and scowled down at her. "Like hell I am! You have no idea what I would give to be with her."

"Clearly not enough." Cassie waited a beat while the argument sank in and a strange feeling rose within him. When he didn't defend himself—wasn't sure how anymore—she spun on her heel. "Fine. Do whatever you want. But be warned that I'm going to have a few things to say to the chief if he's thinking about taking you on full-time."

"Don't worry," Thorne said, "I don't want the job."

And for the first time in the conversation, his words rang with absolute conviction. He thought about standing and squaring off against Maya's friend, or maybe pacing off the restless, unhappy energy that surged through him. But in a sudden bout of self-clarity brought on by his and Maya's fight, he realized that the anger and the pacing was another barrier, another defense mechanism. She'd been right about that, but she wasn't right about the flashes. She couldn't possibly be.

Because if she was right, he wasn't crazy.

He was selfish and blind.

He frowned at Cassie. "Look, you don't want me here and I don't want to be here anymore. So either leave and let me get back to work, or sit down with me and let's figure this thing out. There's something…" He trailed off and tapped his computer mouse, bringing the screen back to life so the timeline shone in plain, boldface type. "There's something here. I just can't figure out what."

After a long, searching pause, Cassie

moved around the desk to join him. But she didn't crouch down to stare at the screen. She stared at him. "Do you love her?"

Startled into honesty, Thorne blurted, "I'm crazy about her."

Cassie sneered in contempt. "More evasions. That's not what I asked. Do you love her?"

Thorne was saved from answering when the phone on her hip beeped and Cassie jolted. She slapped open the unit and scowled. "I hate this phone. How could I have a message when the damn thing never rang?"

"Something to do with cells and roaming, I think," Thorne answered, blunting the unease of her last question by shuffling through the notes on the desk.

He uncovered one in Maya's handwriting.

Too many lines of evidence point toward a current or former Bear Claw cop. Is this intentional? Is the PD the ultimate target?

It wasn't a novel idea or question, but the words echoed at a new level within him as he stared at the computerized timeline.

Hot damn. She was right.

The PD had been the target all along.

He pointed to the screen, to the data that had been bothering his subconscious all along, and turned to Cassie.

She had the phone pressed to her ear. She'd gone pale.

"What's wrong?" he said quickly, heart jamming into his throat when he saw the answer in her eyes. He lurched to his feet with a quick motion that sent her stumbling back. "Damn it, I told her to stay the hell put!"

Cassie flipped the phone shut and headed for the door. "It's not Maya. It's personal. It's—" She broke off and cursed, pausing just inside the door. "To hell with it. You may want to call it crazy, but I know love when I see it." She blew out a breath and said in a low voice, "That was Maya. She's headed out to the Henkes's house on the chief's orders. She didn't want me to tell you. Said it was complicated."

"Not anymore, it isn't." Thorne expected anger and felt only hollow worry, only a big, gaping pit where his heart used to be. "It's all too simple. Come on, let's go."

"Wait." Cassie held up a hand. "I need to find Alissa and Tucker. We'll need backup."

Thorne nodded, but the moment she was

gone, he checked his weapon, grabbed his coat and headed for his car.

To hell with backup. If he was right, there wasn't time for backup.

There might not even be enough time for him to get there.

"HELLO? ILONA? KIERNAN? It's Officer Cooper." Maya rang the bell again, then knocked on the solid oak door that fronted the Henkes home. The pillared gates had glided open as though someone inside had been watching for her arrival, but there seemed to be nobody to answer the door. After a solid five minutes of ringing and knocking, Maya tried the handle.

It gave beneath her fingers and the door swung inwards, gliding on well-oiled hinges.

She hovered at the threshold, her need to hear what Kiernan had told his mother warring with caution. The echoing emptiness of the foyer smacked of a setup.

What if this was an ambush? If Henkes was the Mastermind, then there was no telling what awaited her inside the house. She fingered the weapon at the small of her back, untucked her shirt and pulled it down to cover the gun butt.

"Wait for backup," she whispered to herself, senses alert for the slightest hint of sound or motion from within the house. "The chief is sending someone. They'll be here any minute."

Months earlier, when she'd been officially on the job, there wouldn't have been any question. She would have waited. But her perceptions had shifted in the past few months. Hell, in the past week.

"Officer Cooper?" a voice called from inside the house. "We're in the sitting room."

It sounded like Ilona, sending a wash of relief through Maya, who called, "I'll be right there."

But as she stepped through the door into the opulent foyer, she pulled her weapon and held it at her side, pointed toward the ground. The scene didn't feel quite right. Best-case scenario, she'd scare the dickens out of Ilona and her son with the gun.

Worst-case scenario, she'd need to use it.

She eased across the highly polished marble, her rubber-soled shoes barely making a sound as she crossed the foyer and headed toward the sitting room.

Seeing nothing amiss, Maya relaxed her

guard and strode toward the source of the voice. "Didn't you hear me ring the bell? I—"

She rounded the corner and stopped dead at the sight that confronted her. Ilona Henkes and her son were sprawled unconscious on a Victorian-era couch. Unconscious. Maybe dead. Wet crimson was splashed across the woman's pink silk blouse, and a man was sprawled beneath a nearby upholstered chair. His legs stuck out at odd angles beneath expensive-looking tan slacks, and he wore one loafer, which was barely scuffed on the bottom.

Though his head was turned away, Maya's gut told her it was Wexton Henkes.

It's a setup—get out! Her instincts screamed at her, going into overdrive on a kick of adrenaline and fear. She spun to run, to flee, to get the hell to her car and call in the cavalry. She skidded to a halt when she saw a man's bulk filling the doorway.

"Chief!" she said, nearly squeaking in relief. "Thank God you're—"

Then she saw the gun in his hand and the look of homicidal rage on his face.

And knew she'd made a terrible mistake.

Perhaps a fatal one.

THORNE WAS DOING NEARLY SEVENTY when he turned into the Henkes's driveway. He'd figured on ramming the gates, but didn't need to because they hung open, as though inviting him in.

Bad sign.

He saw Maya's car, saw no signs of violence nearby, but that didn't mean anything. If the Mastermind had planned an ambush, he'd have wanted her inside, so the truth would remain concealed until he decided to reveal himself.

As he slapped the transmission into Park and vaulted from the Interceptor, Thorne acknowledged that the bastard had been one step ahead of the Bear Claw PD all along.

But not this time.

He hoped.

Knowing his arrival had probably been noted, or at least anticipated, Thorne didn't bother with stealth. He marched up the carved granite steps and tried the door. Locked. Knowing the Mastermind would have left it open if he'd meant to make it easy, Thorne didn't bother knocking or ringing the bell. He slipped the pick set out of his inner pocket and went to work on the door, hands far steadier than his heart, which beat an irregular, anxious rhythm, or his brain, which teemed with images of blood and death and a sitting room furnished with expensive antiques.

At the realization, his fingers fumbled on the picks.

He recognized the scene now, and the players. There was nothing left now to do but go through the motions—or rather for the first time since he'd escaped from Mason Falk's captivity, refuse to go through the motions.

This time, he would make his own future. Maya's life depended on it. His love depended on it.

Love. Thorne thought the word without realizing it, then felt the punch of aftershock. He said it aloud. "Love. I love Maya."

Lightning didn't strike him dead. The world didn't end.

Instead, he felt a click of rightness and a stab of bone-deep fear. She wasn't Tabitha, didn't want to exploit a piece of him for her own gain. She wasn't the woman he'd known back at the academy, either. She was stronger and softer at the same time. Determined and dependable. And sexy. So damned sexy it made his bones ache.

Yes, he acknowledged, Cassie was right. He loved Maya. But he hadn't told her so. Worse, he'd left her unprotected, knowing there was no way in hell she was going to follow orders and stay in the condo. Their final parting words had been angry, and for his part dishonest.

He hadn't left her to protect her. He'd done it to protect himself.

And now it might be too late to apologize, too late for them.

"Hell, no," he said, refusing to consider the thought. "He hasn't won yet. He's not going to win. I swear it."

When the lock balked, he touched the knob again on the faint hope that it had come undone. He picked up a flash of dark eyes and dark hair, of a petite woman passing through the same portal minutes—or longer—before. He caught a wash of determination and heartache. He applauded her for the first and felt shame for the second. He'd make it up to her, he promised. He'd spend the rest of his life making it up to her.

If she'd let him.

If the Mastermind let him.

At the thought, he bent to the stubborn lock with renewed determination.

"CHIEF?" MAYA RAISED HER OWN weapon, instinctively squaring off against the man who looked like her superior until she got to his eyes, which were mad. Murderous. Disconnected. Downright scary. "Chief, I want you to drop your weapon and kick it over here. We can work this out."

His lips twisted in an eerie parody of the reassuring smile he'd used to send the task force members to their assignments time and again over the past nine-plus months as they'd sought to solve the Canyon Kidnappings, the Museum Murders and now the new crime wave, which had been orchestrated by—

Maya's brain jammed and she glanced down at Henkes's body beneath the sofa. She didn't see any blood, but he didn't look like he was breathing, either. "Did he come after you?"

She directed the question at the chief, but her mind was racing as too many seeming coincidences lined up into a theory that seemed more bizarre than believable.

Chief Parry snorted. "Don't be naive,

Cooper. We both know what happened here." He used his weapon to gesture at Ilona and Kiernan lying limply on the sofa.

Maya shifted, trying to plan a clean shot that would keep him from harming the others if it came to it, then froze when he returned his aim to her. She licked her lips. "Why don't you tell me?"

Talk to the suspect, Thorne's long-ago voice had said during one of his lectures. An image of him danced at the edge of her mind, casual and long-haired and careless, as he'd been back then. *Stall as long as you can while your backup works into position.*

Only there wasn't any backup. She was on her own.

Thorne, where are you? With gut-deep simplicity, she wished she hadn't let him walk away. So he wasn't perfect. Neither was she.

But their imperfections meshed perfectly. Yes, he tempted her, but in a good way. A strong way.

Why hadn't she seen that sooner?

"I'll tell you what happened," the chief said slowly, slyly as though playing a part, or maybe planning another move. But then his features darkened and his eyes shone with a mad sort of truth. "He was going to shut us down."

"Shut who down? The PD?" Maya tipped her weapon down slightly and eased away from the couch, away from Kiernan, Ilona and Wexton Henkes.

What the hell had happened here?

"Me. The Bear Claw PD. All of it." The chief's face contorted and his voice deepened with fury when he said, "He played off nice to my face and to the cameras, but I found out what he was really up to." He strode to the sofa and kicked Wexton's motionless body. "Bastard. Once he won the election, he was planning on replacing me with someone younger and faster. He was planning on re-imaging the entire PD based on some half-assed study his college roommate did." The chief turned to Maya, and she realized he was too close to her. He leaned nearer to her and brought his weapon to bear. "So I took care of him."

Maya held herself still, forced herself to breathe evenly when she said, "By kidnapping those girls? By killing all those people? How could you?"

He grinned, the expression somehow more frightening than the twisted smile of moments earlier. "By bringing you three in, of course. First I had to get rid of our old crime scene analyst. I talked Fitz into retiring down to Florida because I knew he'd see through me. I wanted you and your friends in the PD because I knew from your records that you wouldn't fit in, that you'd destabilize the force. Disorganize things." His smile gained an edge. "That part of it was even more successful than I'd dreamed. First everyone hated the three of you, and then the other two started sleeping with task force members, confusing things even more. I couldn't have planned it better if I'd tried. When I saw how well that worked, I brought in your old boyfriend. Or did you think nobody knew why you transferred out of the High Top Bluff Academy so lickety-split?"

Maya's mouth went bone-dry and her heart pounded in her chest, in her head, as too many things started making sense. Disillusionment flared. Disappointment. Betrayal. "But you're the chief!"

If the accusation came out sounding weak, it was because she couldn't comprehend his actions. He was a cop. His reputation was sterling. He didn't fit any of the profiles, for God's sake.

But Henkes was on the floor. His wife and child were sprawled on the sofa. And the chief of the Bear Claw PD had his gun aimed at Maya's heart when he said, "Twenty years on the job, and this is the thanks I get? I was trying to fix things, don't you understand? I was trying to protect Bear Claw from Henkes."

"By killing him?" Maya said sharply. She gestured to the body. "If that was the plan, why not just do it? Why did you use Croft and Barnes? Why kill the other people, *innocent* people? How was that protecting Bear Claw?"

Parry's eyes shone with fervid intensity. "It wasn't enough to kill him. Too many other politicians have already bought into his plan. I had to discredit him. Destroy him. Make myself into a hero so nobody could touch me." He kicked Henkes again, and this time got a groan in response. "He's not dead, just drugged. He'll wake up in jail, arrested on three charges of first-degree murder. He shouldn't stay unconscious as long as you did. Your allergy to the drug was…unexpected, though I enjoyed picturing your face when you saw that I'd opened the bottle you kept in your kitchen." His smile turned mocking. "Such a stereotype. The drunk keeping a bottle close at hand. Tell me—did you take a drink once you figured out your boyfriend was really after your job?"

"That's a lie!" Maya snapped before she could stop herself.

"It's the truth. Ask him yourself." The chief chuckled and returned his attention to Henkes again. He prodded the groaning man with his foot. "He'll stay altered for a few hours at most, like Kiernan did when I broke his leg." Parry's eyes swept the three people in the room. Ilona. Kiernan. Maya. He lingered longest on Maya and the corners of his mouth lifted when he said, "Don't worry. I'll see to it that you get a proper state funeral. As long as I can live a hero, I have no problem letting you die as one."

Heart pounding, palms sweating, Maya lifted her weapon. "William Parry, you are under arrest for the—"

There was a flurry of motion. The chief yanked up his weapon at the moment

Thorne burst through the door, shouting, "Maya, drop it!"

"Thorne, it's the chief!" she cried quickly, heart jamming into her throat. "He's the Mastermind!"

"She's insane," Parry said calmly, finger tightening on the trigger of his weapon. "She's already killed Henkes, and was about to go after the wife and kid when I got here. She's had it in for him the whole time because of what she did to that high school kid back when she was married and a drunk."

"Don't listen to him. He's lying. He told me you were only after my job the whole time." Maya looked over at Thorne, her heart jolting in relief at the sight of his strong shoulders and determined expression. But then she saw that the gun in his hand was pointed at her.

And his expression was deadly blank.

I heard the gunshot, he'd said. *I heard you scream and I smelled your blood.*

"Thorne!" Maya said desperately. "Trust me. The chief killed all those people. He told me so himself." His expression didn't change and Maya felt her heart crack in her chest. "I swear it! Thorne, I love you. Do you hear me? I don't care about the job. Not any-more—I care about you. I love you. If you've ever loved me. Hell, if you even like me a little, listen to me. I—"

"You've cried wolf one too many times, Officer Cooper," the chief barked. "This is your last warning. Drop your weapon or I'll—"

Maya turned and lifted her gun, finger tightening as she aimed at the chief's head, knowing it was the only way to ensure the safety of the innocents in the room. The chief raised his own weapon—

A giant's fist slammed into Maya. Pain ripped through her, hot, searing pain that stole her breath and brought darkness. She screamed and spun, and saw an arc of blood follow her.

Her legs crumpled beneath her and she fell.

The last thing she saw was Thorne's face. And the gun in his hand.

Chapter Fifteen

"Good shot," the chief said, his words echoing through the pounding numbness that surrounded Thorne.

A slap of pure rage blasted through his chest, through the barriers surrounding his heart, the ones Maya had penetrated without meaning to, without even knowing. He glanced around the room, at the pricey antique furniture and the signs of a struggle. He saw blood and heard a woman's scream echo in his ears.

Maya's scream.

As he'd foreseen, he'd shot the woman he loved.

I love you, she'd said, trying to make him understand, make him believe. But it had been too late by that point.

No, it had been too late the moment they met. Some futures were immutable.

Thorne nodded slowly. "Yes, it was." Then he lunged at the chief, leading with his fists.

His first punch landed on the bastard's jaw. He felt bone crunch and was glad for it. The attack spun Parry away from the others, and Thorne closed in with a flurry of blows, driving the chief away from his victims.

Yes, victims. Thorne had realized it too late. He should've seen it earlier, should have listened to Maya's suspicions. They'd had it right early on, suspecting that the Mastermind was a member of the Bear Claw PD. There were too many events centered on the department.

More importantly, too many events centered on destabilizing the PD.

Knowing it, Thorne weathered the chief's return blow and drove his head into the bastard's stomach, knocking the breath out of him, sending him flailing backward. The older man tripped over a claw-footed stool and went down hard. The impact jarred the gun from his grip and Thorne kicked the weapon aside. Head ringing with images and pain, Thorne stood over his fallen enemy and leveled his weapon, aiming the business end square between his superior officer's eyes. "I could do it," he said conversationally, the calm of his tone at odds with the wildfire that raged within him.

Do it, his instincts chanted in tones that sounded like Mason Falk's voice. *Do it. He took your woman from you. He took everything from you.*

Parry's face blurred in his mind's eye, becoming that of Donny Greek, who had died at Thorne's hands.

Justifiable homicide, they had called it. Could they really argue that this was any less justified?

The killing rage rose within Thorne as he thought of the lives lost because of Parry's misguided attempt to save his own ass. Because whatever his skewed rationalization, that was what it had been. That, and an unreasonable focus on Wexton Henkes. Thorne bet that if they looked deeply enough into Parry's past, they would find a connection to Henkes, a reason the chief had become fixated on this particular man.

There was another motive here. A woman, perhaps. Money. It usually came down to one or the other. But this time it had spun out of control. The chief had become a victim of his own deluded grandiosity. He'd seen himself as a controller, and had enlisted others in his deadly plan. Bradford Croft. Nevada Barnes. Drew Wilson. God knew, they'd probably find others during the investigation that would lead to Parry's trial.

But why bother? They already knew that the Mastermind didn't deserve to live. Not after what he'd done to Bear Claw.

To Maya.

"I could kill you," Thorne said again, aware of the squeal of tires outside as the others arrived, aware that his window of opportunity was closing. "I've killed before, you know. Nobody would blame me. Not a soul."

Then he glanced at Maya, at the woman he loved. She stirred faintly and moaned with the pain of the bullet buried high in her shoulder. She'd moved at the last moment and he'd caught more of her than he'd intended. Enough so he worried it had been too much.

Fear and regret fisted in his stomach alongside rage. Then her eyelashes fluttered and her eyes opened, clear and brown. Her lips shaped the words, "Don't do it."

He froze, finger tightened halfway on the trigger, gun muzzle pointed at the man who had harmed so many innocents. The chief lay on his back, eyes dark and murderous.

Maya pushed herself off the floor, blood streaming between the fingers she held clamped to her shoulder. Her eyes were steady on his. "Don't do it. I love you."

I love you. The words seeped into him, unfurling an unfamiliar warmth within his chest. She still loved him, even after what he'd done, even after he'd shot her and pretended not to believe her.

"Will you still love me if I kill him?" He forced the words between tight lips, aware of the deadness within his brain, the lack of flashes, of prescience.

He didn't know how this was going to play out.

She held his eyes. "This isn't for me. This is for you. You'll hate yourself if you do it." She pulled herself to her feet, grimacing with the pain, and stumbled two steps toward him to lay trembling, bloodstained fingers on his arm. "Don't do it. Stay here with me. Stay human." She rose on her tiptoes to kiss him on the cheek. "Stay with me."

And he broke. Simply broke. His breath expelled with a rush and he nearly dropped to his knees with the relief, with the love. He kept his weapon trained on Parry, who seemed to have accepted his capture. "God, yes. Yes, I'll stay. I'll stay. I love you. God, I love you."

She smiled, and her heart was in her eyes when she said, "Good, at least we agree on that much."

She leaned forward and kissed him as the others came running in, Tucker first, followed by Cassie and Alissa, then what seemed like the whole damn Bear Claw City Police Department.

They looked shocked to find the Henkes family stirring to fitful consciousness, stunned to find their chief battered and being held at gunpoint.

And not at all surprised to find Maya and Thorne in each other's arms.

Epilogue

The wedding was held in the Bear Claw Creek State Park, late in the summer when the trees and cactuses bloomed with vivid greens and vibrant reds, bold clashes of color that seemed at odds with the stark cut stone of the canyon walls and the wild riot of the rain-swollen creek below. Cassie and Maya wore cactus flower–red and Alissa wore white, as befitted the bride. Moments away from the start of the procession, the wedding party was gathered in a loose knot beyond the flower-decorated archway that led to the seated guests and the final walk down the petal-strewn aisle.

Two members of the wedding party stood aside, enjoying each other.

"It's almost time." Maya brushed a hand down her dress and smiled up at the handsome man standing beside her. "You ready?"

Thorne grinned, a flash of square white teeth that sent a sharp spear of lust through Maya's midsection. They'd been together constantly for the past months, as Thorne had stepped in to help rebuild the Bear Claw PD in the wake of the chief's arrest and subsequent suicide. It had been hard, messy work, and the pieces weren't all in place yet, but they were making progress.

Things were coming together. And Thorne had managed to overcome his aversion to dating a coworker. It was either that or one of them would've had to move, because they damn sure weren't giving up each other.

"I'm totally, utterly ready," Thorne said, his eyes intent on hers, heating when he glanced down at the dress, and the modest glimpse of breast that showed at the neck.

Maya grinned and folded her hands in front of her, using her upper arms to plump her small breasts together and deepen what cleavage she had. "You're always ready for that. I was talking about the wedding."

"Me, too." But he lost his grin when he went down on one knee in front of her, crushing the first of the petals where they spread out from Alissa and Tucker's marital aisle.

As Maya's heart pounded in her chest, threatening to burst through her skin, he pulled a rusty orange leather box with gold embossing out of his tux jacket pocket.

She touched her hand to her throat. "Thorne!"

"It's okay." He nodded toward the rest of the wedding party, where Alissa and Cassie held hands with Tucker and Seth Varitek, the men they had met and come to love during the course of the chief's mad scheme. Engagement bands sparkled on both the women's fingers, evidence of the futures they'd both found with their men. "I asked them and they said it was okay if I stole a bit of their thunder." He gestured at the creek and the blue, blue sky, and at the fallen bit of the canyon where Alissa had found the first of the kidnapped girls, nearly losing her life in the process, and losing her heart instead. "It seemed appropriate somehow, seeing as this was where it all started."

He waved the others forward before he popped the small snap on the leather box and opened the two-sided top to reveal a gleaming platinum band set with three nearly equal-sized diamonds that sparkled like nothing she'd ever seen.

"Thorne!" she said again, shock and giddy happiness robbing her of her vocabulary.

"Maya," he said gravely, but humor flashed in his eyes. "Will you marry me?"

His words echoed back through time but found no comparison to her previous life, to her previous mistakes. She was new now, and whole, and she loved him with all her heart.

She grinned. "Don't you already know the answer?"

"Not this time." A shadow passed across his face. She knew that while he was relieved that the flashes—whatever they had truly been—had left him alone since that scene at the Henkes mansion, sometimes, like during a recent spate of break-ins, he missed the instinct. Prescience. Whatever he wanted to call it. He shook his head. "Nope, I can't foretell this one."

"Well, I can," she said, feeling a smile touch her lips, a lightness touch her heart. "Yes. The answer is yes, I'll marry you."

And then there was no need to say more, because his lips were on hers, and his fingers were on hers, slipping the ring into place as he kissed her and kissed her and the sun gleamed down on them both, warming everything it touched.

A cheer broke out, led by Alissa and Cassie, the two best friends Maya could ever have asked for, and picked up by the rest of the wedding guests, who'd risen from their chairs at the whispered hint that something big was happening.

Soon every member of the Bear Claw PD was on his or her feet, whistling and stomping, and carrying that excitement over when the music came up and it was time for the three couples to march down the aisle, one pair to be married, two pairs to anticipate their own marriages.

And all three couples to look forward to their lives fighting crime in Bear Claw, Colorado.

Together.

* * * * *

Don't miss Jessica Andersen's next gripping romantic suspense. Look for RED ALERT in October 2006, only from Harlequin Intrigue.

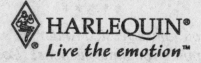

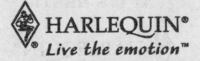

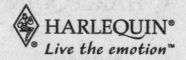

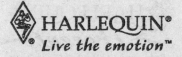

HARLEQUIN®
Presents

The world's bestselling romance series...
The series that brings you your favorite authors,
month after month:

Helen Bianchin...Emma Darcy
Lynne Graham...Penny Jordan
Miranda Lee...Sandra Marton
Anne Mather...Carole Mortimer
Susan Napier...Michelle Reid

and many more uniquely talented authors!

Wealthy, powerful, gorgeous men...
Women who have feelings just like your own...
The stories you love, set in exotic, glamorous locations...

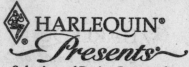

HARLEQUIN®
Presents

Seduction and Passion Guaranteed!